KU-658-907

PLAYING THE
BILLIONAIRE'S
GAME

PLAYING THE BILLIONAIRE'S GAME

PIPPA ROSCOE

MILLS & BOON

All rights reserved including the right of reproduction
in whole or in part in any form. This edition is
published by arrangement with Harlequin Books S.A.

This is a work of fiction. Names, characters,
places, locations and incidents are purely fictional
and bear no relationship to any real life individuals,
living or dead, or to any actual places, business
establishments, locations, events or incidents.
Any resemblance is entirely coincidental.

This book is sold subject to the condition that it
shall not, by way of trade or otherwise, be lent, resold,
hired out or otherwise circulated without the prior consent
of the publisher in any form of binding or cover
other than that in which it is published and without a
similar condition including this condition being
imposed on the subsequent purchaser.

® and TM are trademarks owned and used by the
trademark owner and/or its licensee. Trademarks
marked with ® are registered with the United Kingdom
Patent Office and/or the Office for Harmonisation in the
Internal Market and in other countries.

First published in Great Britain 2020
by Mills & Boon, an imprint of HarperCollins*Publishers*
1 London Bridge Street, London, SE1 9GF

www.harpercollins.co.uk

HarperCollins *Publishers*
1st Floor, Watermarque Building, Ringsend Road
Dublin 4, Ireland

Large Print edition 2021

© 2020 Pippa Roscoe

ISBN: 978-0-263-28837-7

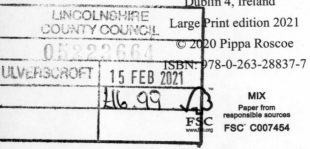

MIX
Paper from
responsible sources
FSC
www.fsc.org
FSC C007454

LINCOLNSHIRE
COUNTY COUNCIL

05223664

ULVERSCROFT   15 FEB 2021

£16.99

This book is produced from independently certified
FSC™ paper to ensure responsible forest management. For
more information visit www.harpercollins.co.uk/green.

Printed and bound in Great Britain
by CPI Group (UK) Ltd, Croydon, CR0 4YY

For Sareeta Domingo,
who saw how much I was inspired
by *The Thomas Crown Affair*
and encouraged me to run with it.

And for Hannah Rossiter,
who helped me to ensure that
it was the best it could be.

My sincerest thanks to you both.

xx

CHAPTER ONE

INTERVIEWER ONE: *Ms Keating, you understand that this interview is being recorded for internal Bonnaire's purposes only and that you do not need a lawyer present?*

MS KEATING: *I'm afraid that hasn't convinced me that I don't need one.*

INTERVIEWER ONE: *But you understand the statement that I have just made?*

MS KEATING: *Yes.*

INTERVIEWER ONE: *Then, if you would, can you please explain how you came to believe that the painting in question was a fake?*

MS KEATING: *As I have already explained, the painting I assessed in Sharjarhere was most definitely not a fake.*

INTERVIEWER ONE: *But you have stated that the painting, Woman in Love, up for auction after a private viewing at Bonnaire's London gallery and damaged on the night of June the twenty-first, was a fake?*

MS KEATING: *[brief pause] Yes. That specific painting was a fake.*

INTERVIEWER TWO: *And you claim that this was a different painting from the one you assessed, certified and valued in Sharjarhere and attributed to the painter Etienne Durrántez, owned by Sheikh Alham Abrani?*

MS KEATING: *Yes.*

INTERVIEWER TWO: *Why is that?*

MS KEATING: *Because I'm very good at my job.*

INTERVIEWER ONE: *We'll get to that later. For the moment, can you explain the circumstances under which you identified the damaged painting as a fake?*

SIA KEATING HAD been breathing hard even before the harsh ring of her phone broke through the nightmare that held her in its grip. She'd been fighting a losing battle with the stranglehold her sheets had around her arms and neck.

Several days later she would wonder if that moment hadn't been prophetic somehow. She'd woken with a feeling of dread. One that seemed to deepen the moment the words reached her from the mobile phone she pressed to her ear.

'Sia, we have a problem.'

Her heart dropped so quickly she wasn't able to form a response for David, the head of Scientific Research. Partly because his nickname in the department was the 'Art Detective' and as much as she liked the bespectacled, calm-toned man, there was only one reason an art valuer got a phone call from him.

'The Abrani painting. It's been damaged.'

Sia flung back the covers and pushed her hair out of her face, concern for the beautiful piece cutting through the fog from her nightmare. 'How?'

'There was apparently some kind of altercation at the gallery.'

'Galleries don't have altercations,' she replied, confused. She cast a look at the clock by her bed. It was two o'clock in the morning. But he'd said the painting was only damaged? If so, then why was David calling *her?*

'They did tonight. But the painting...there's a problem. Could you come down and take a look at it for me? Something's not right.'

For the entire journey between her little studio flat in Archway and the gallery in Goodge Street, Sia's heart pounded with fear. The kind of fear that heralded the termination of careers. David might just as well have proclaimed the apocalypse had come. Because 'something's not right' could really only mean one thing. And as the tube rattled its way along the tracks one thought reverberated in time with the clicks and clacks.

It's not a fake. It's not a fake. It's not a fake.

It couldn't be. The painting she had valued two months ago in Sharjarhere was not a forgery because she double-checked, triple-checked her work. Always. She *had* to.

Sia bit back the mounting nausea swirling in her stomach. For most art valuers, one or maybe even two forgeries were to be expected.

For as well trained as most valuers were, con artists were better, more dedicated, even harder working. They had to be, they got the bigger payout, Sia thought ruefully. Until they were caught.

Sia's mind veered dramatically away from the last time she had seen her father in jail. The way he had looked at her from across the table in the visiting room of Brixton Prison, a sheen glistening in his eyes, his body angled slightly to the side, Sia couldn't help but wonder if he'd purposely arranged himself like a Vermeer. As if everything, his whole life—in *hers*—had been a forgery.

It's not a fake. It's not a fake. It's not a fake.

She ran through the valuation. It had been a bit of a rush as she'd been covering for Sean Johnson, who had fallen ill at the last minute. Even now she felt slightly guilty about the joy she'd felt at having been chosen to replace him *and* the uncharitable belief that his sickness might have been alcohol-related.

No matter how good she was, how accurate, precise and detailed, she'd been passed over for evaluations like this again and again. At first, she'd put it down to being the newbie. Then she'd put it down to being paranoid. And three years in and still missing out on some of the big jobs? She'd been forced to realise that her—or, more accurately, her *father's*—reputation was once again taking its toll on her life.

So she'd been determined to ensure that this valuation was *perfect*. She'd arrived at the palace in Sharjarhere from Athens, where she'd helped her friend Célia d'Argent and Loukis Liordis with an auction that raised an inconceivable amount for charity. Had she been riding so high on her contribution to the charity that she'd missed something at the palace? She shook her head, drawing a slight frown from a fellow tube passenger, even at such an ungodly hour in the morning.

No, she'd gone through each stage of the valuation process: the signature, the artistic style, the paint, the canvas. She'd removed the frame, checked the backing, the details were all correct—variations in the paint levels and thickness, the blacklight showing nothing untoward.

And her gut. The natural instinct she'd been born with telling her that she was in the presence of a true Etienne Durrántez, one of the twentieth century's most famous artists. It didn't matter to Sia that she knew the painting would fetch more than one hundred million pounds. It didn't matter to her who would spend such an impossible amount of money on the painting. It was the painting itself.

The unknown woman stared at the viewer with that same indefinable sense of inner knowledge as the *Mona Lisa*. The secret smile of, as appropriately titled, a *Woman In Love*. The swathe of long dark hair was impressive even to Sia, whose tumble of thick Titian waves were so noticeable she almost always swept them up into a bun at her neck. A slash of red across her lips was worn with pride, not arrogance, confidence, not false bravado, and it had made Sia want to have known the mysterious woman. To understand where her sense of admiration sprung from, not for the painter but the model.

Sia had been so drawn to the painting that there was absolutely no way that it could have been a fake. The signature, the artistic style, the paint, the canvas…she thought, checking through the assessment. And the provenance.

Her breath caught for just a second. She'd

not been shown the provenance. Her manager had informed her that she needn't ask after it because the paperwork had already been forwarded to Sean. And even as she'd begun to question the unusual chain of events she'd heard it. The sigh.

It was one that she'd heard so many times in her three years at Bonnaire's. She could almost picture her manager now. Overweight, red-cheeked and always slightly sweaty, the man practically defined 'old boys club'. It was the kind of sigh that would usually precede some kind of patronising comment about her youth, gender, looks or inexperience.

The rage that had roared in her ears had almost blocked out his disappointment in having to remind her that she had been given an opportunity here and instead of making a mountain out of a molehill she should, essentially, keep her pretty mouth shut and get on with it. Yes, he'd actually said that.

And now, as the tube pulled into Goodge Street station, she was mentally kicking herself for toeing the line rather than following her instinct, trusting her gut. Trusting *herself.*

She held her coat tight against the unseasonal

bite of the night-time gust of wind as she picked her way past takeaway boxes and black bin bags towards the back entrance of Bonnaire's, waved her security pass over the sleek black electric reader and pulled the heavy door open.

Usually, at two-forty-two in the morning the white-walled offices would have been completely empty. But tonight at least fifteen staff were present and through the windows of the glass-lined meeting rooms she could make out at least two company directors, one of whom was shouting into a telephone, the angry words clearly audible from this distance.

Ducking into the stairwell that would take her three floors below ground to the extensive lab that took up an entire level, her heels tapped frantically on the concrete staircase as she ran to where she knew both David and the painting would be.

She ignored the stares of the lab assistants as she went straight to the long bench David used. She glanced to the X-ray room at the back, the red light remaining dark, showing the machine was not in use.

David was at the computer, already going through the images from the infrared and ultraviolet tests before calling up the X-rays. The moment he caught sight of her, he ushered away a few more technicians from where they were staring at the damaged painting and beckoned her over.

The moment she caught sight of the painting she couldn't help the gasp that fell from her lips. Her instant reaction was shock and horror—red streaks poured down the painting, the consistency of wine, but the alcohol had begun to mix with the paint beneath it. Slashes of what had once been raven-black hair now dribbled down the palest of cheeks and the long silver necklace worn by The Woman in Love now pooled downwards towards the painting's frame in a way that most definitely wouldn't have happened if it had been the original painting. The real one. The one that had been valued at over one hundred million pounds.

'It's fake,' she exclaimed.

'Yes.'

She collapsed into the chair in front of the painting. 'This isn't the painting I valued. David—it's not. I wouldn't have made that mistake. Have you checked the photographs from my file?'

David paused before leaning against the table, facing her with a grim expression.

'I...they haven't given me access to the file.'

'But that's...' Sia trailed off. 'How are you supposed to evaluate against the initial assessment?'

'Sia, look, I think you should know that—'

But Sia wasn't hearing David. She was looking at the small video capture in the bottom of David's computer screen.

'What's that?' she interrupted.

David cast her one last concerned look before turning back to his screen.

'Security footage from the incident. It looks as if two guys got into a bit of a fight near the painting.'

Sia was unable to prevent her hand from pressing against her lips in shock at the sight of the fight that had broken out between the two men, causing a glass of wine to be thrown with unwavering accuracy against the painting.

'Is that Savior Sabbatino?'

'Yes, and his brother Santo.'

Sia bit back her shock. The Sabbatino brothers were more likely to be seen on the cover of a scandal rag rather than security footage. The implications of the damage to the painting, the seller and the gallery were beginning to spin beyond the realms of imaginable.

'Can you go back?' she asked David of the footage. Something was niggling at her and she couldn't quite tell what it was. She watched the footage again and again—the wine hitting the painting, the shock rippling out not only from the Sabbatino brothers but the attendees of the private viewing as each person turned their head, watching with horrified fascination the damage to such an expensive piece of… piece of…

There it was again. It was precisely because he was the only person in the whole room who didn't turn his head. Instead of being drawn to the moment like a driver passing a car accident, he had his back turned and was taking a sip of his drink with something that looked, to Sia, like the ghost of a smile.

It was a man she would have recognised any-where. Just like any other red-blooded woman, whether or not they had a penchant for billion-aires with bad reputations.

INTERVIEWER ONE: *So you immediately suspected Sebastian Rohan de Luen?*

MS KEATING: *Sheikh Alham Abrani was very clear in his instructions. The painting would never be sold to Seba—Mr Rohan de Luen. He had made many offers to purchase the painting in the last ten years, all of which had been far above the asking price, and had been refused each and every time.*

INTERVIEWER TWO: *Mr Rohan de Luen is a duke, is he not?*

MS KEATING: *His father was the Duque de Gaeten in Spain before being stripped of his lands. However, because this happened after Seb—after he had been titled at the age of eighteen, he was entitled to the... well, to the title, I suppose.*

INTERVIEWER ONE: *But on the night you believe you discovered the painting was a fake, he had not been anywhere near it?*

MS KEATING: *He was present at the private viewing.*

INTERVIEWER TWO: *But the CCTV footage shows that throughout the entire evening he was nowhere near the painting. In fact he remained behind to give a witness statement to the police, who were called in case any charges were to be brought against the two gentlemen involved in an altercation that damaged the painting.*

MS KEATING: *Well, he would hardly hold up his hands and say, Me, me—I did it, would he?*

INTERVIEWER ONE: *[clears throat] And when you took your concerns to your superiors...?*

Sia could feel the nails of her fingers pressing crescents into the softness of her palms and knew they'd leave a mark.

'But I've told you, this is not the painting that I valued in Sharjarhere.'

She'd gone straight from David's lab to the executive offices, five floors above. She didn't know what she'd expected, but her manager's response was not it.

'Ms Keating. Please, I'd love to hear what is

more plausible. That you were mistaken in your valuation or that you valued a true Durrántez, which was then somehow stolen and replaced with a fake painting on the way to Bonnaire's London gallery, which was then so unlucky as to have been damaged in a one-in-a-million altercation that caused wine to be spilled on it?'

Sia wasn't stupid. She knew what it looked like, could understand it seemed an almost unbelievable chain of events, but she knew what her gut was telling her. And, she cursed silently, she knew that she would never have valued a fake painting. It was the only thing that her father had given her before his arrest and incarceration. The ability to spot a forgery from a mile away.

'If I could just share the photographs I took in Sharjarhere with David then—'

'We have already spoken to Sheikh Abrani, who has apologised profusely for any confusion.'

Sia frowned, because she doubted if the determined, overly confident and deeply arrogant man she had met when evaluating the painting had ever apologised to anyone in his life. There was simply no way he would have admitted to even accidentally attempting to sell a fake Durrántez.

'But—'

'The file has been sealed and will remain that way until we can finish our internal investigation. And until then, Ms Keating, you are being placed on suspension, during which time you will not speak to anyone—*anyone*—of your suspicions. You will have no contact with either Bonnaire's staff, the press or the Duque de Gaeten.'

The blood drained from Sia's face. Suspension? No contact with her colleagues? Sealed file? None of this was making any sense whatsoever. She could understand why Bonnaire's might want to keep the damage of a painting—even a fake one—quiet until they had been in contact with the seller and the prospective buyer. But they had already spoken to Abrani. Everyone had decided that the painting was a fake, but they were wrong. The painting *had* been stolen, the thief was getting away with it and the only person being punished was her.

Her already dented reputation and her very young career were at stake. Everything that she'd worked so hard for. Everything that she'd fought for.

She closed her eyes, refusing to allow the tears she felt pressing against the back of her eyes to fall in front of her manager. No, she'd learned a long time ago not to let them see her cry.

At first it had been her aunt, who had never liked the fact that her seven-year-old niece was being foisted upon her while her wayward sister lurched from one man to another in the wake of her husband's imprisonment. The strict, dark and deeply conservative home of Eleanor Lang had been a short sharp shock to a little girl who'd been given pencils and pens and all but told to 'have at it' on the walls of her father's studio. How on earth was a seven-year-old to know that there was a significant difference between the white paper her father had spread across his studio walls and the magnolia paint that covered her aunt's sitting room and hall-way?

After that, it had been the children at school. Her hair would have been target enough had the newspapers not been full of photos of her father—the most notorious art forger in England. Ever. Mothers refused to let their children near her, and teachers eyed her as if she would steal the shoes from their feet if they didn't watch her closely enough.

And while her aunt had given her food and board, there was little money for anything else. So when Sia hadn't had her head in her books, feeling an illicit pang as she traced her fingers over images of paintings she had once seen her father delight in copying, she had held down two after-school jobs, knowing that, whatever shape her future would take, it would have to involve university. Because it would have to be *proper,* it would have to be beyond reproach. It would have to be something that no one could take away from her.

But they had taken it away from her. Even when she'd followed the rules. Done everything perfectly and absolutely right. As the reality of her suspension began to sink in, so did the maths. She might have held down two after-school jobs as a teenager, but her university education had cost her greatly. She had debts of nearly twenty-eight thousand pounds that her position at Bonnaire's had barely managed to scratch the surface of. And even a month's suspension could seriously damage her credit history, let alone her housing.

As nausea rose in her stomach, the grainy black and white image of Sebastian Rohan de Luen, smirking into his whisky rose in her mind. She knew that he was involved as sure as she knew a real painting from a fake. And she was going to do whatever it took to prove it.

INTERVIEWER TWO: *So, despite direct orders from your manager, you approached the Duque de Gaeten.*

INTERVIEWER ONE: *[low laugh] And how did that go down?*

It had taken Sia less than twenty-four hours to decide her course of action and track him down. The man had a social media page that was as effective as Google Maps, so it wasn't finding him that had taken the most time. No. It was finding her courage. Her plan was simple. Seduce him, find the painting, steal the painting. Or re-steal it anyway. Sia tucked her morals away on that front. Because surely it couldn't be illegal if she was returning stolen property?

No, she decided. It wouldn't. Even if she did benefit from it. Because surely if she returned the painting, the *real* painting, she would prove that she hadn't made a mistake and Bonnaire's would reinstate her. She would *prove* that she was good at her job.

That she was nothing like her father.

She shook the thought from her head as she approached what looked to be just another row of impossibly rich houses in Mayfair, each fronted with two Ionic columns either side of a sleek, shiny black door with a bronze lion's head door knocker. In fact, only the door with the large suited man in front was in use as, beyond the door, the partitions between the houses had been knocked down and the entire row had been converted into one of London's most sought-after private clubs.

When she'd discovered where Sebastian would be she'd known that she'd need help. No way would she have been allowed within fifty feet of the place—even with her surname. But her friend Célia on the other hand… Even before she'd married Greek shipping tycoon Loukis Liordis, Célia had a company with a reputation that would have opened many doors, including this one.

'Even if I get you in, *chérie*, you're going to have to look the part. And, of course, you always look incredible, but you need to look… *rich*.'

Sia's heart had sunk a little at her friend's declaration.

'This is important, *oui*?'

'Yes.'

'*D'accord…*'

Two hours later Sia had walked, wide-eyed, towards the green domed doors of Harrods where she met a lovely woman called Penelope who had been instructed to provide her with a complete outfit, hair and make-up for that evening and discreetly send any bill back to Célia.

She'd spent the next three hours in a complete daze. Dress after dress were given to her to try on, each one more beautiful than the last. When she had first conceived of her harebrained scheme she had imagined herself in black, her hair pulled back into an efficient bun at the nape of her neck, her make-up simple. Something espionage-ish.

But now, as she looked down at the slash of

silk peeking through the rich cashmere coat, she felt a tendril of excitement. Penelope had described the dress as teal and Sia had bitten her tongue. It wasn't teal at all. The colour was more closely Prussian blue, her—and her father's—favourite colour. She'd never once worn it, but when she'd seen in the mirror how well it complemented her pale skin and made her light auburn hair glow like gold she'd been speechless.

The stylist had batted Sia's hands away when she'd insisted on having her hair up and then accused her of committing some great crime, which had made Sia blush more than necessary. So she'd sat back and let him have her way. Sia's hair had been spun into large, seemingly careless waves that softened features that she'd been told far too many times were 'strong' in a way that clearly meant 'masculine'.

By the time she'd reached the suited man by the sleek black door of Victoriana she'd half convinced herself that all of that preparation had been for nothing and she'd be turned away, despite Célia's involvement, and was almost breathing a sigh of relief that she could simply go back home and curl up on the sofa, when the man greeted her by name and the door swung open, inviting her in.

She bit her tongue as she was greeted by a young woman dressed in a pair of tweed breeks and a contrasting waistcoat over a white shirt. Sia found herself looking around for a riding crop, such was the effect. Victoriana indeed.

Sia's coat was taken and she was led down the corridor towards what could have been called a drawing room but was so large that the word simply didn't do it justice. Along one side was a marble bar that stretched the entire length of the room. Behind it stood barmen and women, dressed similarly to the girl presently guiding Sia towards a seat, who was explaining the different rooms spinning off from the hallway behind, words like *library, billiard room, morning room, orangery*...all of which disappeared into the gentle hum of the conversations of the people.

Sia soon found herself deposited into a beautiful mahogany stool lined with a worn green leather seat at the bar, in front of a man looking expectantly at her with a broad smile.

'What's your poison?'

Sebastian Rohan de Luen, she thought.

The barman interpreted her silence as confusion and pressed on, not unkindly, with another question. 'What flavours do you like?'

'Ginger. Rum,' she decided. Not usually much of a drinker, Sia decided that some Dutch courage wouldn't go amiss. But she would stop at the one. Because instinctively she knew that she would need *all* her wits about her.

While the barman created her cocktail Sia scanned the room, trying not to show her surprise at the number of famous faces she saw. A TV star sat with the male model currently gracing Piccadilly Circus's illuminated advertising boards. A politician was pressing far too closely into someone he really shouldn't have been, and a news presenter was having a heated debate with a foreign dignitary.

But all of them faded into the background the moment that she caught sight of the tall, dark figure in the far corner of the room, bending slightly as if to hear what the beautiful woman he was talking to was saying.

She had found the Spanish Duke, but felt as if she were the one in the trap—not him.

She couldn't pull her eyes away. It was as if she'd been set alight and was painfully conscious of everything—the feel of silk against her skin, the gentle hum of voices around her, the way that the light glinted on the large red jewel on the necklace of the woman he was talking to. But, aware as she was of all those things, nothing was more prominent than him.

His profile was powerful. The faint trace of stubble marked a proud jawline, framing his features, and matched the thick waves of burnt umber coloured hair on his head, making her hands twitch reflexively. Even in the shadowed lighting of the corner where he and his companion stood, she could see the almost honeyed colour of his skin, rich and tempting. The exquisite cut of his clearly expensive suit outlined broad shoulders, a flat stomach and firm thighs. And, for the first time in what felt like for ever, she itched for a sketchpad. She wanted to trace the outline of his features, copy them, fill the page with the impression of...

She saw him still. It was an almost imperceptible absence of movement probably unnoticeable to anyone, but she had been so focused on him it blared at her like an alarm.

Unerringly, Sebastian Rohan de Luen, lifted his head and gazed directly into her eyes. Her heart missed its next beat, her breath caught in her throat and she nearly cursed when she saw the same ghost of a smile she recognised from the security footage from Bonnaire's.

He might be the most handsome man she'd ever seen, he might own a dozen four-star hotels around the world, he might be titled, but he was also the man who had singlehandedly destroyed her career and her future.

And she wasn't going to let him get away with it.

CHAPTER TWO

INTERVIEWER ONE: *And you say that he approached you?*

MS KEATING: *Is that so hard to believe?*

INTERVIEWER TWO: *If you could just answer the question.*

MS KEATING: *He approached me.*

SEBASTIAN ROHAN DE LUEN, raised the cut-crystal glass of whisky into the air, clinking it against the champagne flute, and relished the feeling of pure unadulterated pleasure running through his veins.

'To a dish best served cold,' he proclaimed, before taking a very welcome mouthful of ice-cold peaty alcohol. 'I couldn't have done it without you, so thank you.'

He looked into a pair of dark eyes outlined with thick kohl and most likely devastatingly attractive to anyone other than him. But he'd known Aliah for far too long and for that entire time they'd been united by one goal to the exclusion of all else. And that had clearly altered the usual dynamic he engaged in with women. Objectively, she was incredibly beautiful, but...

No. Nothing.

'And I wouldn't be here without you, so thank *you*,' Aliah replied sincerely.

'Dare I ask what you're going to do with your new-found freedom?' Sebastian asked before taking another sip of his drink.

'I have some business to attend to.'

'How suitably cryptic,' he observed wryly, genuinely uninterested. They had both played their part. Now it was time to...

'And you?' Aliah's melodic voice slid into his thoughts. 'Back to Siena? Or will you be visiting Maria while you're in town?'

Sebastian couldn't help the way his lips curved into a smile at the thought of his younger sister. Even if she had recently done the last thing he'd ever expected and run off with a Swiss billionaire on the eve of his best friend's engagement party.

'Maria has found herself a husband and is

presently living on the edge of Lake Lucerne,'
he managed to say without betraying his dis-
trust of Matthieu Montcour, his *very* new
brother-in-law.

'Oh. That's lucky.'

'Is it?'

'Some might say. Is she well?' Aliah asked,
her genuine interest for his sister lessening his
anger for the moment.

'She's nearly eight months pregnant, so I'm
guessing that she is.'

'That's wonderful,' she said, and Sebastian
didn't miss the note of longing, or the slight
sheen that dusted the edges of her dark eyes.
'Uncle Sebastian, now that is a sight I'd like
to see.' Aliah's smile was both mocking and
envious, the shadows hinting at the unhealed
wounds from the recent separation from her
own family. 'Indulge them and appreciate
them,' she commanded.

'I do,' Sebastian replied honestly. 'That is
why it had to happen now,' he said, his grip
momentarily tightening on the thick glass. 'Before Maria's child is born. A fresh start and the
past behind us.'

'I'll drink to that,' she said, gently tapping the rim of her glass against his.

As the amber liquid burned down his throat Sebastian wondered if that feeling of peace would come now that everything was as it should be. A feeling that he'd been chasing for ten years that nothing and no willing woman had been able to appease.

With his father finally settled with his step-mother Valeria in Rimini, each happily making the other's life a living hell, and Maria with Matthieu Montcour, it felt as if it was the first time that he'd had no responsibilities. The world was his oyster. His hotels were doing incredibly, the opening of the Caribbean flagship was less than a week away—an event that would allow him to wrap up all loose ends from the Bonnaire's situation. Maybe then he'd find that sense of...

'I lost you there for a minute,' Aliah said.

'Never,' he replied, forcing a smile to his lips as it came time to say goodbye. 'If you ever need anything, I mean it. Anything. Let me know.'

He leaned forward to let her kiss him on the cheek. It was a chaste kiss from a friend.

And it was most definitely *not* responsible for the sudden slap of adrenaline and arousal that cut through him when he looked over Aliah's shoulder and caught a glimpse of the woman sitting at the bar, her gaze locked onto him like a laser beam.

'Seb?' Aliah asked, the husky tone of her voice barely cutting through the power of whatever it was that had him in its grasp.

Ignoring her question, he stared deep into the pair of startling blue eyes as they clashed with his and he felt it like a punch to the solar plexus. For a moment he simply felt awed. A rich, almost terracotta-coloured swathe of gentle curls poured over slender shoulders and dropped almost halfway down pale-skinned and very toned arms. Silk in a regal blue sheathed a body from neck to ankle that made his mouth water. For all of the scantily clad women Sebastian had encountered in the last ten years, this one was the definition of modest, but she alone held the power to undo him. And when his eyes returned to hers, to take in the arch of high cut cheekbones and a mouth made for sin, he couldn't help but pause. There was something about her... And then it dawned on him.

Oh, he was in trouble.

And he couldn't for one minute bring himself to regret it.

Because this? This was going to be fun.

Sia barely noticed the waiter place her drink before her as she watched the Duke return to his conversation as if her entire world hadn't shifted on its axis. Forcing her eyes away from him, she turned to the drink and blinked at it for a moment, having quite forgotten what she was supposed to be doing.

A blush rose to her cheeks and she hated it, hated *herself,* for in that moment—the brief pause before he'd smiled—Sia had forgotten everything. The potential loss of her job, the stolen painting, the fact she was sure that Sebastian Rohan de Luen, was at the heart of the entire mess. No. For that brief moment she'd been struck by an attraction so powerful that she'd almost forgotten her own name. A mistake, she promised herself, she'd not make again.

Reaching for her drink and letting the sweet spicy taste wash her lapse of judgement away and the sharp sting of alcohol bring her back to the task at hand, she realised that she hadn't counted on him having company. Stunning company at that. Casting a quick glance back towards the darkened corner where the handsome couple were still discussing something discreetly, she couldn't help but appreciate the woman's beauty. The way his body was angled beside her was almost protective and for a moment Sia tasted the bitterness of jealousy on her tongue. Not for her, or him, but what they seemed to share. There was something vaguely familiar about her, but Sia couldn't quite place her. It was hardly surprising that a man with Sebastian's roguish reputation was with a celebrity of some sort.

Frowning, she thought over her plan which, she now saw, had more holes than a sieve. What had she been thinking? That *she* could play *him? Seduce* him even? The blush returned to her cheeks with a vengeance and embarrassed tears threatened at the corners of her eyes.

And that slight blur to her eyes was the reason she didn't immediately notice that the Duque de Gaeten had crossed the room and come to stand beside her.

'It's a crime.'

The sensual tone of his voice rippled across her skin but it was the words that sparked outrage in her heart. Which was why it took her a moment to gather herself, to stifle the fury welling within her, before she could respond. That this man chose to refer to a crime... Did he know who she was? Was he playing the same game as she? A thin blade of anger cut through any concern. It made her mad. It made her bold.

'What is?' she asked, no trace of the heat in her veins or the pounding of her heart.

'For a woman as beautiful as you to be sitting alone.'

'The greater crime, surely, is the badly delivered line which has left me feeling somewhat cheated. I had expected more from, reportedly, the most renowned playboy in all of Europe.'

'Renowned? You have me at a disadvantage. You clearly know me, at least by reputation.'

'Henri.' The name slipped from her tongue as if it hadn't been more than twenty years since she'd been called by it. And when he repeated the name back to her, as if feeling the word on his tongue, it sent shivers down her spine.

'You don't look much like a Henri.'

Perhaps she didn't. But Sia knew one thing very definitely. Sia Keating would never be able to do such a thing. Sia Keating was the good girl. She didn't put a foot wrong, never complained, never spoke out, was never angry... Anger was passionate and passionate was too much like her mother. But Henri? Her father's nickname for her, the shortened form of her middle name... Henri might just be able to pull this off.

'Oh, really? What *do* I look like?'

My downfall.

Thrusting aside the errant thought, Sebastian cast a long, slow pursual from the golden halo of her hair to the point of her diamond-encrusted blue heels and back again. He knew that the gaze was insolent and tried to cling to that feeling instead of succumbing to the simple desire to relish her. She was exquisite.

He challenged any man to refute the allure of her hair. Stunning long, honeyed, golden tendrils fell in waves down her back. This close, he could see that her make-up was subtle, allowing an incredible innate beauty to shine. The sheen from the silk glowed beneath the subtle lighting of the room, the shadows showing the shapely outline of her legs, crossed at the knee, legs that were so long Sebastian thought she might actually stand face to face with his six-foot frame. The slash of silk across her collarbone perfectly displayed a long elegant neck and the sleeveless cut showed off arms that were slender but shapely. There was a concealed power to both her body and the whip-smart mind he could tell was running through myriad possibilities and reactions to the words that would next come from his mouth.

It had been on the tip of his tongue to say something crass. It was what she expected of him, it was exactly what he'd set himself up as being, but then he caught the look in her startling blue eyes.

There, beneath the false bravado, because it clearly was false, was something else. Something that pierced a conscience he professed not to have. It was too much like the way his sister had looked at him—not that there was anything brotherly in his thoughts about the woman in front of him. No. But it was the vulnerability beneath the defiance. It was worthy of more than he had planned to offer her.

'*Biondina,*' he eventually replied.

Obviously the same pale skin, auburn hair, but there was also something similar about the eyes. Not now, not from the moment that he'd come to stand beside her, but before then. Just after he'd said goodbye to Aliah, setting her on the path towards a much happier future than she'd ever been offered by her father.

He'd stood watching the way a golden curl swept down her arm as she reached blindly for her drink. He'd wanted to know what she was thinking, because her mind hadn't been on the present, he was sure of it.

'Excuse me?'

'By Frederic Leighton,' he answered, returning to the present at her question.

'I know who painted *Biondina.*'

The offence in her tone, the pure indignation, pulled his lips into a broad smile. 'Oh, do you work in the arts?' he asked, all mock ignorance. The tease was too easy for him, and she was a terrible actress who seemed only to remember after the fact that she wasn't Sia Keating.

There was something in his tone…something that made Sia feel that he might be toying with her. Playing her even? If he had stolen the painting, then in all probability he would have researched Bonnaire's. It was a possibility she hadn't had the time to think through before now and if she had then, rather than letting her tongue run away with her, she might just have owned up to being Sia Keating in the first place. But she'd said Henri and now some deeply hidden sense of mischief was winding within her. The desire, the need to challenge him. To *best* him.

'I work for Bonnaire's,' she said, watching closely for his reaction.

'Isn't that some kind of art dealership? Like Christie's?'

Mentioning their main competitor was just mean and, despite her suspension, she couldn't help the bloom of loyalty unfurl in her chest.

'Yes, but better,' she replied condescendingly—a tone she didn't think she'd ever used before.

'Wasn't there some kind of scandal there recently…?' She watched, fascinated, as he clicked his fingers twice as if trying to remember. 'Ah, I know. Didn't a painting get damaged at an auction?'

She was so surprised that he'd taken the conversation there that no words came.

'Or was it a fake? Or was it both?' He shrugged, the smile on his face seemingly one of bemused ignorance, yet to Sia it was like a red rag to a bull...until Henri took over, transformed the fire of helpless fury striking her silent into determination and action. She matched his tone and manner, joining in with the playful flirtation with the truth.

'Both apparently,' she said easily. 'Though may I tell you a secret?'

'Of course,' he replied, leaning in as if for her to confide.

'I don't think it was a fake,' she mock whispered behind her hand. 'At least, not before it was stolen and replaced with a forgery,' she concluded.

'Now that *would* be a scandal,' he said, as if impressed by the idea. 'Though I can't imagine for one minute an art house with a reputation like Bonnaire's would be willing to admit to such a thing,' he all but taunted.

Behind her smile, Sia's jaw was clenched with anger. Because he was right. They weren't. And that was why she was there, engaging in some

insane cat and mouse game with an international playboy. Sia would have walked away,
but Henri dug her heels in. Henri was the girl
who had drawn on walls, who had laughed until
she'd cried with her father, who had dressed up
in the beautiful turquoise silks her mother had
left all over their home in Peckham, who at
the age of six had worn bright red lipstick and
walked in too large high heels. It was time to
see what she could do now as an adult.

'I'm surprised that a hotelier has his fingers
on the pulse of the international art scene.'

Sia had to bite her lip to keep the smile from
spreading, seeing the outrage that crossed Sebastian's features at the word 'hotelier' and
at how easy it had been to pierce that clearly
healthy ego of his.

'My hotels are four-starred, the restaurants
have Michelin stars, celebrities beg to stay in
my penthouse suites. I have one in every major
European city, more off the beaten track inter-
nationally and at least two that are so exclusive
they are not even known to the press, one of
which is on an island.'

Despite herself, and the arrogance with which
the information was delivered, Sia was im-

pressed. Because, if the articles she'd managed to read online before coming here tonight were right, Sebastian's family had been exiled with little more than the clothes on their backs.

'And Leighton comes into this...?' she asked, as if bored of his list of achievements.

For the first time since he'd appeared at her side, Sebastian seemed to bite his tongue. 'Family heirloom.'

'You had a Leighton as an heirloom?' she blurted out, unable to keep the awe from her tone or prevent her eyes from widening.

'We had a couple,' he said, shrugging, as if they'd just been lying about the house.

'Anyone else I should know about?' she asked, almost forgetting the game.

'My father had a penchant for the Italian Renaissance—Giotto, Fra Angelico, Filippo Lippi... But my...mother preferred twentieth century artists. Rothko, Klee, Francis Bacon.'

Sia was so awed at the idea of growing up with authentic paintings by the artists he'd named, she'd missed the way that he'd stumbled over the reference to his mother. Without realising, he'd evoked her childhood fantasy and she imagined walking down grand mahogany hallways with the masters hanging on every wall. But she couldn't prevent herself from asking, 'Etienne Durrántez?'

'Amongst others,' he replied, without taking his eyes from her. She'd been watching closely for any sign, the smallest of movements, but there had been none.

Had she got it wrong? Before making the call to Célia she'd spoken to an old university friend who'd gone to work at Interpol. She'd not heard anything on the grapevine about a stolen Durrántez, and clearly Sebastian had no need for the money. She couldn't even begin to fathom why he might have wanted the painting. But he clearly had wanted it enough to make several public and incredibly generous attempts to buy it. Though she'd not found any record of him trying to buy any of the other Durrántez for sale. There must have been something in particular about *that* painting.

'I have a table. Would you care to join me?'

Sebastian half expected her to say no and half resented the slight burst of adrenaline he felt when she inclined her head and gestured for him to lead the way. Sebastian might have recognised her but, beyond knowing that Sia Keating had been sent by Bonnaire's to Sharjarhere as a last-minute replacement to evaluate the Durrántez, he knew nothing. There'd been little or no point doing a check on her by that stage. Besides, she was sure to be just as corrupt as the rest of them. She'd arrived at the palace, done her job and left. If he'd known for even one second that she'd be as feisty, playful and smart as she'd proven herself to be in just a short conversation he might have done things a little differently.

Because she was proving to be a worthy adversary. An adversary it would be worth knowing a little more about.

Victoriana had been a favourite of his ever since he'd leased his apartment in Mayfair. Very few people knew about either the club or his apartment and he liked it that way. His sister had liked to think that she was completely independent in her little flat in Camberwell, and Sebastian knew how important it was for her to feel that way. But he'd been looking after her since she was eight years old and he wouldn't stop just because she'd wanted to come to London for art school.

He caught the eye of one of the staff, who nodded in return and proceeded to lead them to a more private area of the members only club. He gestured for Sia or Henri—he sensed there was something about that name that gave her confidence somehow—to precede him and when he, in turn, joined the procession he instantly regretted his courtesy. The demure high necked dress's secret caused him to inhale sharply. From how she'd been sitting, he'd not seen this angle before and now it caused an arousal so acute he was momentarily wordless and witless. The silk fell from her shoulders into a deep cowl that apexed at the base of her spine, revealing inches and inches of smooth creamy skin and showing clearly that Sia was bare beneath the silk. His mouth watered and he clenched his jaw against the need he felt coursing through his veins. And if the gentle sway of her hips was anything to go by, she knew exactly what kind of effect she was causing.

He knew from previous visits that he had approximately forty steps to get his raging libido under control before they would be directed to their table and he was going to need every single one of them. Because, instinctively, he knew he'd need all of his brain cells to tackle the dilemma that was Sia Keating.

They were shown into the Orangery, which would during the day look out onto an exquisite garden, cultivated and completely secluded. But, at this hour of the night, the outside was nothing more than a deep dark cocoon held at bay by the glass panes encased in white painted leadwork. Fairy lights hung from the ceiling, reflected in the windows, creating a canopy of thousands of stars above them.

The garden had been brought inside with hanging baskets of strings of pearls, strings of hearts, long trailing ivy and many more vivid bursts of green, the names of which Sebastian could hardly guess at. Every time he came in here, it never failed to impress him. But, within the large high space, there was more that really drew the eye. Huge bird cages in distressed white, old forest green and black, of all different shapes, some classically rounded at the top, some square—one even had tiers and a swinging perch—filled the space. Ivy grew around the ironwork, winding through and around the bars of the cages, giving the people inside them a feeling of privacy and secrecy.

Large enough to fit tables and chairs, some even large enough to fit groups of eight or ten, they were quite incredible and, from the look in Sia's eyes, almost the very last thing she'd expected. They were shown to one of the smaller cages, with cushioned seats on either side of a small round table clinging to the curve of the bars.

Two glasses of champagne were placed on the table and the discreet waiter disappeared. As she took one side, he took the other. Sebastian couldn't shake the feeling that they were combatants on opposite sides. Because he didn't think for one minute that it was a coincidence that she had referred to Durrántez, using a name which he knew to be fake, appearing the same night as he in a private club when he knew her salary would barely cover a drink, let alone membership to Victoriana.

Oh, Sebastian knew *all* about the backroom deals Bonnaire's pretended not to do and he'd hardly been surprised when the Sheikh had chosen them to fence his ill-gotten painting.

But the moment the Sheikh had agreed that the painting had been a fake all along, Sebastian thought it done and dusted. Victory in his grasp. Revenge against Abrani for him and the others.

The last thing he'd expected was for Bonnaire's to send in some Mata Hari in a blue silk dress.

'We were talking about art. I'm curious,' he said, and he meant it, 'what is it that you *value* in an artist?'

Sia tried to prevent the tug of a frown at his choice of word. Surely it was her imagination. But as her mind picked over the possibilities her subconscious supplied a word that surprised her and spoke far too much of a past she wanted to leave behind.

'Authenticity.'

'A woman with a good eye then,' Sebastian returned without missing a beat.

'I'll take that as a compliment from a man with a good eye.'

The smile that broadened his lips was pure sin and Sia was horrified to find that she liked it.

'My friend?'

'She is truly beautiful,' Sia replied honestly. 'As are you.'

It took everything in Sia to hold his gaze. To not shrug off the easily given compliment, shy from it or deny it.

'You don't think so?' he asked, sounding genuinely intrigued and cocking his head to the side as if observing something fascinating.

'I think it is irrelevant in the presence of a beauty like hers.'

'Ah. Well, impartially, I can see your point but, as an old family friend, I do not quite see the allure. To me, your beauty shines brighter than anyone else in the room.'

And Sia hated that his assurance took the bite out of the strange nauseating jealousy she'd felt swirling in her stomach. But it did make her plan easier, not to have to compete with another woman.

A plan she was seriously beginning to doubt. And, for just a second, she allowed herself to wish that this was as simple as what it seemed to be: a handsome, charming man finding her interesting and beautiful. It was a yearning that took her by surprise. Sharp, sudden and acute.

She'd never had time for boys or, later, men.

At school her goal had been university, desperate to get away from the cold, staid clutches of her aunt's house. And at uni? Just feeling the money slipping through her fingers each moment she was there had been enough to forge a single-minded focus she'd not really ever let go of. So she'd spent her Friday and Saturday evenings in the library and her nights alone in her bed and if it had made her feel a little lonely then so be it. Because she'd got her degree and a job that she loved for the most part and she was happy.

It was the touch of the pad of his thumb across her cheek, the way that his finger angled her jaw that brought her back instantly. It sent a cascade of sparks across her nerve-endings, lighting her pulse and kicking an extra thud into her heart. For just a moment she hoped he would kiss her. At the look in his eyes as he gazed at her mouth, she fooled herself into thinking that he might want to.

'Eyelash,' he said by way of explanation, pulling the rug from beneath her.

She couldn't do this. There was something about Sebastian Rohan de Luen that was more than just the arrogant playboy art thief and that made him dangerous. Too dangerous.

'I should go.'

CHAPTER THREE

INTERVIEWER TWO: *After all that, you just left?*

INTERVIEWER ONE: *I don't understand. You didn't even ask him if he stole the painting?*

MS KEATING: *But Bonnaire's doesn't think there was a painting to steal.*

INTERVIEWER ONE: *No...but you do. That's why you were there, isn't it?*

MS KEATING: *Yes.*

INTERVIEWER TWO: *So why did you—*

MS KEATING: *If you would let me finish?*

SIA COULDN'T EVEN look at Sebastian.
'I should go.'
'But do you want to?'
Yes. No. She honestly couldn't say any more.

He'd levelled her with such a look, one that she felt down to her toes. It was one that spoke of challenge and temptation. Sia would have run for the hills, but Henri? While Sia was a combination of all the things that had happened *after* her father's arrest, Henri was all the things from before. The passionate, reckless, thought-less parts of her mother and the intensely fo-cused, creative, calculating parts of her father. Henri had been locked up for far too long and now she wanted to play.

She felt the sharp sting of arousal as his gaze locked onto her lips and desire rushed through her bloodstream, reaching parts of her body she barely recognised. She both welcomed and feared it, torn between the two. Never before had she felt such a thing.

'What I want has very little to do with it.'

'How strange,' he said, cocking his head to one side as if to inspect her from a different angle. 'I don't think I do that very often.'

'Do what?' she asked, genuinely confused.

'Self-restraint.'

The arrogance with which he said it, the sheer ego of the statement itself made it near impos-sible for Sia to keep her mouth closed against the shock. But she couldn't help the question that fell from her lips.

'You don't have self-restraint?'

'It's not that I don't have it. It's just that I don't need it.'

It was as if she had been drenched in ice-cold water. Any thread of attraction she thought she might have felt had been effectively doused by his...she internally growled...infuriating arrogance. Was this why he thought he could take the painting? Because he *could*? Because there was no reason that he could see *not* to? Given all the things that it had cost her, she was fuming.

She took a sip of champagne from the glass on the table between them to buy herself some time. She was so mad she could have walked away. And quite possibly would have, had it not been for the suspicion that it was exactly what he'd intended her to do.

Sebastian could see that it was working. He might have intensely disliked pretending to be the pampered, pompous playboy but it was better than what had passed between them moments before. When he'd touched her cheek with the pad of his thumb and felt a shower of fireworks across his skin.

It had been enough. Enough to know that whatever it was between them, it needed to stop. Especially if he was to find out what it was that *she* wanted from him. Because for a moment there he'd wanted to kiss her almost as much as he'd ever wanted the Durrántez. And that was inconceivable.

He took a sip from the champagne flute and looked around the Orangery. Anything to momentarily dull the impact of Sia Keating's stunning beauty. Was it only a few months ago in Paris that his best friend, Theo Tersi, had accused him of being jaded? Sebastian nearly choked on a laugh at the memory of it. He'd imagined it would take a few more years of indulging in a debauchery he'd welcomed with open arms a scant three years ago.

Though Sebastian wasn't sure what the Greek billionaire vintner would make of his current situation. Especially since Theo had developed something horrifyingly close to a moral code since he'd married and now had a child on the way. And not just a child, but a *royal* child. Who would have thought it? Theo Tersi, husband to a queen, soon-to-be father to a princess.

Still, although Sebastian had not exactly been lying when he'd told Sia he didn't need self-restraint, it didn't mean he was unfamiliar with the concept. In fact, he'd been overly familiar with it from the age of eighteen when his world had broken apart and his father had refused, or been incapable, of doing a single thing about it. Having spent his late teens and early twenties pulling his family from the ashes of financial ruin that had crashed down upon him and his sister Maria with such suddenness it felt as if nothing would ever be real and lasting in his life ever again, he had spent the following few years amassing an empire that rivalled anything the Dukes du Luen had ever before seen in the history of their nobility. During that time the fact that he'd also provided a roof over his father and stepmother's heads and a quite intentionally separate roof for him and his little sister, for whom he'd all but become a guardian, had left him feeling that he deserved to let off a little steam.

So he had. In whatever way he'd wanted, with whomever he'd wanted.

Although admittedly in the last few months, ever since the masked ball in Paris he'd accompanied Theo to, he'd not indulged. Perhaps that was why Sia Keating was having such a dramatic impact on him. Not because there was anything significant about her specifically—other than her beauty, of course—but simply because it had been quite some time since he'd lived up to his debauched reputation.

If he wasn't careful, he'd end up like Theo. Married and with a child on the way.

Just like his little sister.

But he *was* careful. He'd shouldered enough responsibility to last a lifetime. There were just three people left on his list until this whole Bonnaire's thing was completely resolved, and then it would be just him. Free to do as he wished, completely. And he chose to ignore the image that flashed in his mind of Sia Keating in a pool of royal blue silk sheets.

Which was presumably the only reason the question he asked came out of his mouth.

'What do you do for fun, Henri?'

* * *

I honestly don't know, would have been Sia's reaction. But Sebastian had asked Henri, so she answered.

'You mean besides having a drink with a notorious playboy?'

'Are you trying to tell me that you've had drinks with *other* notorious playboys?'

This time the mock arrogance and outrage in his tone lifted her lips into a reluctant smile. Because, for some reason, for all its apparent mockery, his reaction had felt so much more real than his insistence that he had no self-restraint.

'Are there so many of you?' She dramatically shuddered. 'Women be warned.'

'No, I can assure you. There are none like me.'

And Sia was beginning to think that he was right. There was something about the directness of his gaze, the way that his features almost seemed to relax when he was telling the truth. As if thankful for the brief respite from having to hold a mask constantly in place.

Sia turned her attention back to the question, feeling a slight ache in her heart as she did so.

When was the last time that she'd had fun? When had she laughed until she'd cried, when had her stomach ached with joy and her chest heaved with an air so light it could have been helium rather than oxygen? Since she'd taken the job at Bonnaire's she'd worked all hours she could, desperate to prove her worth. To prove that she wasn't her father. Her salary hadn't left much over after rent and travel, food and basics. The offset was that she travelled with work, she supposed—Sharjarhere, Greece, Istanbul, New York to name just a few. But in that time the few friends she'd gathered from school or university had gone their own ways. A few work colleagues had stuck—Célia in particular. But she was now happily married and working on starting a family. But even with Célia it had been a close friendship, but perhaps not one based on fun exactly.

'It hurts that you have to think so hard to answer that question.'

Sia looked up to find him studying her once again, but this time sincerely, not for show, with his head angled towards his shoulder. She couldn't quite take the whiplash change of direction their conversation was taking. One moment full of tease and taunt, the other full of painful introspection.

'It is getting late. You have responsibilities? Work in the morning, I would imagine.'

The query hit a little too close to home. It felt a little as if he were pushing her, taunting her as if somehow he knew about her suspension and, despite the notion being fanciful, she couldn't help the bitter words which fell from her tongue.

'And what would you know of responsibilities?' she bit out, the acidity painful on her tongue.

He shrugged his shoulders. 'Very little. After all, apparently I'm the most notorious playboy in Europe.'

'So humble.'

'I don't believe in humility.'

'Really?'

'In most it is a lie and in others it is simply the desire to be considered worthy which, in itself, is hardly humble. I have neither the need to lie nor the desire to be considered worthy.'

'Because you don't think yourself worthy?' Sia asked, genuinely curious.

'Because I don't care how people consider me.'

'Not even the most beautiful woman in the room?' she asked ruefully.

'Oh. I *know* how you consider me,' he said with such a self-satisfied smile she had a strong urge to wipe it from his lips.

'And what would that be?'

'You consider me overly arrogant, purposely obtuse, careless and thoughtless. But I'm incredibly handsome, you can't help but be entertained by my charm and you're curious to see if there's a deep well of inner turmoil that could possibly redeem me.'

Well. He had her there.

'May I tell *you* a secret?' he asked, seemingly intent on using her words against her. She nodded and stilled as he moved towards her, one arm braced against the bar and the other at the back of her chair. As he leaned in, his lips close to her ear, she breathed in an aftershave that made her mouth water and her pulse race.

'There isn't,' he whispered, sending a chill down her spine as he promised no redemption.

As enticing as it was—the promise of hedonistic, irredeemable pleasure—she didn't fully believe it. So, before he could lean back, before she could question her own intention, she turned her head ever so slightly, and this time it was her lips at his ear when she whispered, 'I don't believe you.'

'Really?' he said, leaning back and questioning her. Although the smile was steady on his lips, there was a dark shadow twisting in his eyes.

'Yes,' she said, locking her gaze with his. 'I'm very good at spotting fakes.'

The accusation struck a nerve he honestly didn't think he had. It made him angry. Oh, he'd been called fake before, but not in the sense that she had meant it. That Sia Keating, of all people, might just have seen behind his carefully constructed façade was untenable.

But, if he was being honest with himself, it wasn't her words that had struck deepest. It was that moment when she had turned to him, her lips barely a second from his and he'd wanted so much to take them with his own, to press against them, feel them, taste them.

Which was the only conceivable reason for him to say, 'You're not the only one, Sia.'

He watched as her head jerked back slightly as if she'd been struck and clenched his jaw against the wave of guilt. He abhorred violence against women, even verbally, and although no harsh words had been spoken a gauntlet had been thrown down. And now he'd started he just couldn't stop. 'But being able to spot fakes is a nice touch, given your occupation. I have to say, Bonnaire's has gone up in my estimation, sending such a tempting morsel my way.'

'I don't know what to be more offended by. Being described as a "morsel" or your assumption that I'm here because of Bonnaire's. I assure you, Mr Rohan de Luen I am here for myself.'

'I may have been exiled, but I'm still a duke, Ms Keating,' he said with all the imperiousness he didn't feel in that moment.

'Forgive me, *Your Grace*, a slip of the tongue,' she said insincerely.

He stifled a growl of arousal before it could reach the back of his throat as his mind suggested colourful displays of what he would very much like to do with her tongue.

'If you are here for yourself and not on Bonnaire's business, then why the use of a fake name?'

'If you knew it was fake, why entertain the deception for so long?' she quickly returned.

He could have pushed for an answer to his question—part of him wanted to, but now was not the time. Instead, he answered hers. 'Perhaps I wanted to see how far you would take it.'

'All the way,' she replied, determination flashing in her eyes.

'And, just so there isn't any misunderstanding, what does that look like to you?'

'To prove that you stole the painting.'

'Ah,' he said, for a moment regretting the images her accidental double entendre had thrust into his mind. 'The painting which I believe Sheikh Abrani has himself stated is a fake?' The careless tone of his own voice was barely audible over the pulse pounding in his ear. Bonnaire's, the Sheikh...they had done as expected. Hidden within the lie and taken the hit. But Sia? Now the gloves were off and she'd admitted her true intention—an intention that went far beyond what he'd have expected a corrupt Bonnaire's employee to have admitted. If the painting had been valued by Sean Johnson this wouldn't have been a problem at all. But Sia

Keating was a new player and as such all the more dangerous for them all.

'But it wasn't,' Sia ground out, repeating her insistence that the painting she'd valued wasn't a fake.

'And you are sure that you didn't just make a mistake?'

She scowled and Sebastian thought that for a moment he saw more than just professional ego shimmering in her eyes.

'Very. You stole that painting and replaced it with a forgery. I have absolutely no idea why you would then have arranged for the painting to be damaged in a way that revealed the whole thing, nor why Abrani would claim it to have been a fake all along. And, to be honest, I don't care. But I *know* you did.'

'How?' he asked, genuinely curious.

'In the last ten years you have made twelve offers for that painting. Each one has been turned down. You have shown zero interest in any other Durrántez painting, yet *this one* clearly holds a fascination for you. At the private viewing, of every single person there, you alone did not watch in fascinated horror the damage being done to a painting valued at one hundred million pounds. And why? Because you knew it wasn't worth even a fraction of that.'

'That's what you've got? A hunch and the fact that I was more interested in my date than a painting?'

'It's enough for me,' she said mutinously.

'Good for you. But what is it that you think you can threaten me with? You can't go to the Sheikh—he has admitted to owning a forgery. You can't go to the police. No one has reported a theft. And the fake painting was damaged before it was sold, so no crime has been committed,' he concluded, shrugging his shoulders.

'I could go to the press,' she said, anger sparking in her eyes like fireworks.

'And you'd just look like someone who is trying to cover up a professional mistake through desperation and lies,' he said in a tone that was painfully patronising to his own ears.

'I could steal it back.'

He ground out a laugh and, as he expected, it ignited the rage within her. 'You'd have to find it first.'

'You think this is funny?' she demanded.

He hardly did, but he needed her to think that.

'I've been suspended. So you didn't just steal a painting, Your Grace, you stole my job, my career, my future. Everything that I've worked towards for my entire life.'

Sebastian felt as if he'd been slapped. Bonnaire's had sent probably the *only* person with integrity to Sharjarhere and because of him she stood to lose her job. Guilt fought with his own personal need for justice and in that moment Sebastian had the horrible feeling that there was no way that they would both walk away with what they wanted.

He could have sworn in that moment that he felt the tide of injustice wash against him from where she sat. Injustice, betrayal, loss. He knew those words. Knew that anger.

'So if it takes me a year—ten years—I'll find the proof. Because there's *always* proof. You didn't do this by yourself, you couldn't have. I will track down everyone that helped you, every single person you've spoken to in the last six months. I will visit every single place you've been in the last six years. If you try to move the painting I will know about it. If you try to sell the painting I will hear about it. You might be a billionaire businessman with contacts around the world, but I have lived and breathed art since I was born. And I will use every single contact I have to make sure that I get my hands *back* on the real Durrántez.'

'That's quite the speech,' he commented drily despite how impressed he was. While part of his mind worked through the implications of her words, the other recognised just how incredible she had become in that moment. It was as if with the challenge, in her desperation, she had risen from flames and become a phoenix—glorious, golden, bold beyond belief and utterly enthralling. Everything in him wanted to reach for her, to hold her to him, to clutch that power to him.

Everything apart from the fact that if she did as she promised it wasn't just he who would pay the price. Each person involved had known what the implications were. Each person had made their decision freely. But they had also put their faith in him and his plan. The plan he'd assured them would come off without a hitch. Never would he let anything happen to them because of the one truly selfish thing he'd ever done.

Sia Keating uncrossed her legs and stepped

from her chair around to the opening in the cage. It felt oddly like a portent of things to come. Unable to stay behind, he stood and met her head-on. Something primal roared within him and satisfaction uncurled in his gut as she stood, as he'd predicted, almost face to face with him.

'I am going to find out exactly what happened, who helped you and tell the world,' she promised him, golden sparks firing in her eyes captivating him as she stepped past him.

Once again, the sight of her backless dress taunted his arousal. The incredible pride stiffening her shoulder blades made him smile in appreciation even as he thrust all thoughts of expectation from his mind.

He reached for her wrist, encasing it firmly but gently, and pulled her back round to face him, cutting off the view that had sent him into a sensual torment.

'You're playing a dangerous game,' he said, his tone darker and harsher than he'd intended.

'You started it,' she replied, but there was nothing childish about the huskily delivered accusation.

That he really couldn't deny. Nor could he

any longer ignore the only possible solution he'd been able to come up with. It was risky, but it could work.

'I have an offer.'

'You think you can buy me off?'

'Why would I need to buy you off?'

'Because you stole the painting.'

'I haven't said that I did. But neither can I have you running around making such accusations. It's not exactly good for business,' he sniffed, aiming for both nonchalant and irritating.

'Which business? Art thief or hotelier?'

'If I am guilty of your accusation, then both, I would assume.'

He could practically feel her frustration crashing against him like the tide. Good. Perhaps she'd be so incensed that she'd agree to his crazy proposition. Despite the fact that he was making this up on the spot, Sebastian had always been a goal-orientated quick thinker. This was what he was good at and what most people, who believed the carefully constructed careless playboy façade, took for granted. Thinking through the options, there was only one sure-fire way to know just how dangerous Sia Keating was.

Keep your friends close and your enemies closer.

'What if I gave you fourteen days?' he asked.

'Fourteen days of what?'

'Unfettered access to my life. Twenty-four hours a day for fourteen days, and if—at the end of it—you have not found your proof then you give up. Walk away and never think of it again.'

'Two weeks?'

'You should consider yourself lucky. Two days is my usual tolerance for female company.'

'I'm not your usual choice of female companion,' she returned so quickly he had to suppress a smile.

'I'm beginning to see that.'

'And if I *find* proof? Find the painting?'

He smiled, dark and predatory. 'If I am inept enough an art thief to leave either proof or painting lying around for you to find, then you are welcome to them.'

Sia couldn't believe what she was hearing. Not only did he clearly believe that she was incapable of doing what she'd said, he was also teasing her with every word. She fisted her hands so hard she knew she'd leave crescent marks in her palms. She wanted nothing more than to prove him wrong, prove him guilty.

She wasn't stupid. She knew that she didn't have the funds or the contacts to investigate him with the same depth as he was suggesting. But neither was she naïve enough to think it would be that easy.

'What does this "access" entail?' she asked cautiously.

'You can accompany me wherever I go. You can be by my side for business meetings and events, breakfast, lunch and dinner if you wish.'

'You said twenty-four hours a day...' The question came out of her mouth before she'd had time to properly think it through.

'You are more than welcome to join me for the nights, Ms Keating. My bed is big enough, I assure you.'

'As is your ego, clearly,' she bit out.

Rather than being bruised by the put-down, Sebastian seemed instead to relish it.

'My properties are large enough. There are plenty of spare rooms. That is, if you don't trust me not to do a midnight flit with the stolen painting.'

'I don't trust you as far as I can throw you.'

'Wise, Ms Keating, wise,' he warned.

'Which is precisely why I don't believe that you would make it this easy for me. What is stopping you from simply lying your way out of this? What makes this better than me investigating on my own?' she demanded.

He seemed to give the question, and her, some thought. His eyes assessed her once again—not the heated open perusal of before but more thoughtful, calculating—and it made her feel worthy.

'I'll allow you one question a day that I will answer with complete truth, no matter the question.'

'Just one?' she asked, buying herself some time, surprised by the addendum to their deal.

'It's more than I've given any other woman in my life.'

And she believed him. She hadn't been lying when she'd told him that she could spot fakes and forgeries. Her childhood had been built on it. Her career had been defined by it. And now her future would depend on it.

This was her only chance. It was more than she could have hoped for really. She wouldn't have been able to sustain Henri's persona for more than one night. It was too...tempting? She shook that thought away and focused on what Sebastian was offering.

'Okay. I'll do it.'

'It will mean a large upheaval of your life for the next fourteen days,' he cautioned.

'That...won't be a problem,' she replied, heat still simmering across her skin from her suspension.

'No...husbands or lovers to get insanely jealous and come after me with a pitchfork?' There was a teasing tone in his voice but his eyes held no spark of humour, only dangerous curiosity.

'No, but it's worth noting that I have my own pitchfork.'

'Good for you.'

His apparent support only infuriated her more. 'You don't want your lawyers to draw up any legally binding documents?' she asked, slightly surprised that he hadn't demanded she sign a million non-disclosure agreements.

'I'm happy with a gentleman's agreement.'

'You are hardly a gentleman.'

'Then perhaps *your* lawyers would be so obliging?'

Her silence said enough.

'Thought as much.' From his pocket he removed a sleek white embossed card and offered it to her. In a glance she took in the address and contact information for Sebastian Rohan de Luen.

'Then I will see you at nine tomorrow morning.'

She felt his retreat from the room the way that warmth dissipated as the sun set and her fingers closed around the stiff card in her palm.

Game on, Sebastian. Game on.

CHAPTER FOUR

INTERVIEWER ONE: *So, let me get this straight. The Duque de Gaeten, invited you to...what? Live with him for two weeks and you said yes?*

MS KEATING: *Yes.*

INTERVIEWER ONE: *After you told him you believed he'd stolen the painting?*

MS KEATING: *Yes.*

INTERVIEWER ONE: *Knowing that you were looking for proof of the stolen painting?*

MS KEATING: *Yes.*

INTERVIEWER TWO: *[sotto] What was his house like?*

INTERVIEWER ONE: *[clears throat]*

INTERVIEWER TWO: *[louder] I mean, in which of his houses?*

SIA LOOKED UP at the mansion in front of her with a strange sense of déjà vu from the night before. Once again, she was looking at a shiny black door with a bronze door knocker, only this wasn't a lion's head, it was that of a stag.

She could still back out. She didn't *have* to do this. Only…he had taken everything from her. She'd put her past behind her and stepped towards a new future. If she didn't prove to Bonnaire's that he had stolen the painting, that she had been right, she would never work in the industry again.

She'd lost so much. She refused to lose this too.

Which was why she found herself being led down a black and white checked marble floor towards a lower level of the Knightsbridge townhouse by the uniformed butler who had answered the door. Whilst still trying to hide her natural disapproval towards Sebastian for having an honest-to-God butler, she frowned a little as the air began to turn warm and she could have sworn she caught a faint trace of chlorine. She followed the butler into the room beyond the door and the scent dramatically increased as she inhaled a gasp of shock.

The butler retreated with little acknowledgement of her surprise, apparently used to such a reaction, leaving her standing beside a pool the colour of a cloudless summer's sky. The entire basement seemed to have been covered in sandstone, up-lit in a way that made it feel both warm and secretive. Along the length of the pool, the stone curved into arches with lush green vegetation that veiled the faint traces of chlorine somehow.

The sound of lapping against the edges of the pool drew her attention back to the water to where she could see a powerful shape gliding towards her. She was speechless as Sebastian broke the water of the deeper end of the pool, thrusting wet hair away from his face, his eyes—almost the same colour as the water—locked on her without shame or embarrassment or even any intent that Sia could discern, making her even more uncomfortable. He placed his hands on the side and drew himself out of the pool with the kind of grace that she was envious of. And then she had no thought for grace.

The last time she had seen a man in a swimming costume it had been on Brighton beach, their shorts had been baggy, their legs were like twigs and definitely turning that particularly British shade of burnt.

In tight-fitting thigh-level shorts Sebastian was none of those things. Well used to assessing pieces of art, her eyes went to work over every single inch of his body. She couldn't help but watch as water dripped from the hair he had swept back, onto his shoulders, running over muscles that spoke of more exercise than just swimming. She followed its progress over the dips and turns as it fell over pecs and abdominals that made her ache to touch. His hips were tapered just slightly, but not too much, making her deeply aware of his masculinity. She tried to retain objectivity, observe purely professionally, but she just couldn't. She might have studied the human form more than most doctors, followed the direction of paint across scenes of sensuality so incredible they'd been preserved for hundreds of years, traced her hands over cool marble sculptures...but she'd never seen this much of a man in real life and couldn't help but blush. It was almost painful as it spread over her cheeks and she bit her lip from…what, she honestly couldn't say. He was overwhelming. And by the time she raised her eyes to his, sparkling with more than a little awareness, she knew he knew it too.

'We like to keep the temperature warm in here,' he said, reaching for a towel, still not breaking eye contact, 'for obvious reasons. There are costumes you can borrow any time you like.'

'I'd rather not wear your girlfriend's cast-offs,' she replied, surprising herself with the acidity in her tone. But Sebastian? No, he seemed to find her response amusing.

'The costumes are for guests. My girlfriend wouldn't need one,' he said, turning and offering her a view of his back that made her want to dig her nails into the defined musculature there. She tried to shake off whatever spell he'd cast on her as he wrapped the towel around his waist.

'Breakfast?' he asked, walking past her back to the door towards the main part of the house, his bare feet leaving quickly drying watermarks where he stepped. She suddenly had the strange desire to place her own foot within the imprint, to follow in his steps, to slip into this strange world of butlers, indoor pools and swimming naked that was most definitely not hers.

Sebastian was aware of Sia behind him as he stalked through the halls of his London apartment. It had never bothered him before, going straight from the pool to breakfast, he'd never cared that his feet were bare, his skin half dry, his hair still wet. But there was something about Sia...so buttoned-up and fully clothed that he was conscious of it all. Not *self*-conscious— no, his ego was far above such things. But he still reached for the white robe that his butler had left for him beside the table where breakfast had been placed.

He'd hoped that last night he'd imagined it. The power her beauty had on him. Tried to convince himself that it had been a trick of the light, or the shock of her intention, even the challenge that she presented. But no. It was still there. That unwavering sense of...electricity, energy arcing between them. And he couldn't tell if she could feel it. Sometimes it seemed that she could and sometimes not.

He gestured for her to sit before he took his own seat. He ran his eyes over the breakfast table. A steaming pot of coffee, fresh fruit, croissants, a selection of meats and even a few boiled eggs. He nearly laughed. He wondered what Sia would say if he told her that he usually just had toast.

He doubted that she'd believe him.

'Coffee?' he offered. He was already pouring her a cup before she'd nodded her agreement.

'So, is this what you do all day?' she asked. 'Swim, eat and luxuriate?'

'You want to know what I do?' he asked and, in doing so, pointed out the rather presumptuous, slightly defensive tone of her question, before playing right into her preconceptions. 'As little as possible.'

Which, of course, was a lie. He'd worked through the night, finishing only at six that morning, dealing with a crisis in the Hong Kong hotel. In truth, he was exhausted, running on fumes and his hundredth cup of coffee in the last eight hours. Not that he would let her see that for a second.

Sia, in contrast, looked like a breath of fresh air. She wore a crisp white buttonless V-neck shirt tucked into high-waisted, wide-legged blue wool palazzo trousers. Given that, perhaps she had just been hot in the pool room. He got the distinct impression these were her work clothes. They were high quality and looked good on her—they'd have to, of course, especially if she were meeting sheikhs, royals, billionaires and whoever else might have their hands on hundreds of millions of pounds' worth of art. But they didn't necessarily feel like her.

He had to drag his eyes away as she reached for the coffee. The sight of her slender wrist, skin that had seemed pale in the pool room now, in the natural light, looked like honeyed cream, and thoughts of the deep tan of his own rough skin next to hers nearly unmanned him.

Instead he focused on the small holdall at the doorway to the room.

'Is that all you brought?' he asked without thinking.

It was the absence of movement that made him realise. Most people moved, flinched, reacted to a wound—verbal or otherwise. Sia seemed different, but in her silence he heard her response like a shout. *It's all I could afford.* And he felt like an ass.

'I'd like to look around.'

He gestured for her to do so and Sia was surprised. 'You don't want to…' she shrugged '…give me a tour?' The idea that she'd be let loose in his home was both a surprise and slightly frustrating. 'I can just thoroughly investigate the entire apartment?'

'I have nothing to hide,' he said, taking a sip of his coffee.

'*Here.* You have nothing to hide *here*,' she replied, unable to keep the disappointment from her voice.

He quirked an eyebrow in question.

'You have, as you've been quite proud enough to declare—a large number of hotels around the world, at least three residences, one in London, one in Siena and the other in New York. It is highly unlikely that you would offer me complete access if you had the painting here. However, in case you are attempting a double bluff, I'll just take a turn,' she concluded as she pushed back out of her seat.

'By all means. And when you are done investigating, Benjamin will show you to your room. In the meantime, I have some very important luxuriating to be getting on with. But if you need me, I'm yours.'

His last words repeated on a loop in Sia's mind as she made her way up the ridiculous amount of steps in the five-floor mansion that Sebastian called his London apartment. Despite her words about a double bluff, she knew he'd never offer her access like this if there was even a hope that she'd run into the painting. So it was unlikely that was here.

But as she walked the hallways lined with expensive art collections, priceless antiques and furniture, her disappointment gave way to awe, which in turn gave way to confusion. It just didn't feel like him. It was incredible but staid, old, *moneyed*. It didn't speak of the charming, game-playing playboy. There was no sense of *fun* in the décor. She had half expected to find a painting from the *Dogs Playing Poker* series hanging on the wall in between a Rembrandt and a Vermeer, but there wasn't one.

And all this space… What did one person *do* with it? She pushed open another door into another empty bedroom. Each one was perfectly made up, clean, immaculate, as if waiting to be filled, and suddenly it struck her as a very lonely house.

Down another flight of stairs, the smooth curved banister cool beneath the palm of her hand, and it looked just like the two floors above it. Barely taking note of the impressive paintings on display any more, Sia wondered if Sebastian had grown numb to their beauty in the same way she felt herself becoming, and almost laughed. Less than a few hours in his world and she had stopped caring whether the next painting was a Picasso or a Degas. Though, even as she thought it, she peered around, hoping that it actually *might* be a Degas.

Smiling at the turn of her own thoughts, she pushed open a door that she quickly realised was not like the others. The sheets on the bed weren't turned down with almost military precision, but were crumpled in a heap. The pillows still bore the impression of being recently slept on, and the air still held the scent of aftershave that was unnervingly familiar. A sound should have drawn her attention to the slightly open doorway in the corner of the room but she couldn't tear her eyes away from the impossibly large bed. She was in the midst of calculating just how many people it might be feasible to get on it when the flash of something at the edge of her sightline drew her gaze.

Once again, the man had a towel around his waist and far too much delicious skin on display. His muscles rippled as his arm towel-dried his hair and the breath caught in Sia's lungs.

'We really must stop meeting like this.'

She practically squeaked as she fled the room in a burst of shocked frustration made only worse as Sebastian's laugh chased her down the corridor.

It was strange having another person in his house. He never entertained his female guests here, despite what he'd said to Sia in the pool room. So, having Sia move independently around his space left him feeling...out of sorts. He'd been halfway through his dinner when he'd realised that she might have wanted to join him, his food sitting uncomfortably in his stomach until Benjamin informed him that Sia had asked to have her dinner in her room.

Reluctantly, he had to concede that he really

hadn't thought this through. Yet it had been the only way to ensure that the people who had helped him—who *he* had helped—had his protection as much now as ever. So, reaffirming his conviction in his decision, he'd instructed Benjamin to invite Sia for a drink.

And as Sebastian looked out across the London skyline from the luxurious roof terrace, he turned his mind to the puzzle that was Sia Keating. He was surprised that she hadn't yet asked her question. He'd thought it might have been the first thing she'd say to him. She was clearly gutsy enough to have approached him in Victoriana, even to have accused him outright of the theft of a painting worth over one hundred million pounds. But she'd blushed like an innocent in the pool room, and run from his room as if the hounds of hell were on her heels. And the only real distinction between the two had been the use of the alias Henri.

'It's a beautiful home you have here.'

Still dressed in the same white shirt and wide blue trousers, there honestly didn't seem to be a wrinkle or hair out of place as she walked towards where he sat as the sun hovered lazily on the horizon as if reluctant to leave.

He stood, gesturing for her to take a seat at the table opposite him. Her eyes seemed to soften momentarily at his manners, until his response checked hers.

'This isn't my home.' He hadn't meant for it to sound so sharp. It gave away too much and she knew it.

'Then what is?' she asked as she sat in the seat, briefly smiling at Benjamin as he poured her a glass of wine.

'Is that your question?' Sebastian asked as Benjamin retreated.

'Not the one you have agreed to answer truthfully, no.' Her eyes settled on his with a confidence he found somewhere between Sia and Henri.

'My primary residence is in Siena,' he said, answering her original question. 'It was the first property I bought after leaving Spain.'

'Do you miss it? Spain?'

There was a pause while he chose whether to answer her or not.

'Yes. It is a strange thing to know that you will never be allowed to go home.'

'When was the last time you were there?'

'I was eighteen. My father made a bad choice of who he wanted to go into business with. But he also convinced a few other noble families, and not just in Spain, to invest in the same deal. So when the deal...fell through we weren't the only ones to lose everything. The shame it brought, not just to our family or the other investors, but the royals was immense. And because my father was the main investor and the one who encouraged the others to follow his lead, we were exiled.'

The bare facts did not convey what had happened but he could not stop the images from that night pouring into his mind. He felt the shock of it all over again. Remembering how men had come to his home, ripped things from the rooms and the walls, while Eduardo had sat in his chair, glass of wine in hand, ignoring Valeria, who was screaming obscenities at him. Maria had been standing at the top of the stairs in her nightdress, scared out of her mind, not knowing what was going on. Sebastian had practically shoved the men out of the house while they'd threatened to come back with the police and legal documents, which he'd told them to do.

Realising that his father was incapable of doing anything, there had only been one way forward. In less than twenty-four hours Sebastian had contacted lawyers, taken inventory of all their estates and what was left after the Spanish government had seized their property. With the help of a few remaining staff, he'd got Maria packed and told Valeria to take care of herself and her husband, as a man ticked off the only items they were allowed to leave with—possessions from their mother's estate from before she'd married Eduardo.

Not that they'd remained with the family for long. Over the next few months Sebastian had been forced to sell everything that wasn't nailed down. The only thing he'd kept was for Maria—their mother's necklace, which she never took off. He'd kept nothing for himself. In part because there'd been only one thing he'd wanted from his childhood and, nearly twenty years later, he'd finally got it.

'It was hardest on Maria,' he finally said, his voice gravelly as if roughened by tension. 'She was only eight when it happened. Having to leave her friends, her school…it was difficult.'

* * *

Sia felt an empathy with his sister. She herself had been seven when her entire life had changed. But she couldn't help wondering...

'And what about you?' she asked.

'Is *that* your question for today?'

'No,' she replied, oddly frustrated with the constraints on their conversation.

She felt his eyes on hers for a moment before he turned to take a sip from his glass—a red, she noted, while she had white wine. She watched as his throat undulated as he swallowed a mouthful of the rich alcohol, strangely hypnotised by the movement. She'd known that, until Benjamin had arrived with Sebastian's invitation, she'd been hiding. Even now she felt a blush threaten to rise on her cheeks at the memory of Sebastian in his room, at his presence even now.

The evening's gentle breeze soothed her heated skin and she looked out across a skyline of London she'd never seen in person before. Above the table was a crisscross lattice with clematis winding through it. Large oldfashioned light bulbs gave off a gentle glow and the large terracotta pots of shrubs and sweet herbs worked to make her forget that she was in the heart of one of the world's busiest cities.

'Why Henri?' he asked, pulling her back to the present.

Sia thought about not answering, just like he had, but she needed him on side for when she did ask her question.

'Henri is short for Henrietta—my middle name. My father used to call me Henri when I lived with them.'

'What happened for you not to be living with your parents?' he asked, the light of curiosity shining bright in the blue depths of his eyes.

'You mean you didn't have someone behind the scenes run up a file on me?'

He shrugged. 'Where's the fun in that? We have fourteen days in which you are determined to thoroughly investigate me. Perhaps I could do the same.'

Something she chose to ignore arced between them—a kind of energy, or electricity even—but it faded into the background as the realisation that he might not know who she was began to dawn on her.

'You really don't know?' she asked out loud. The narrowing of his eyes was the only response he gave, clearly not enjoying being in the dark. 'My father was John Keating.'

The narrowed eyes turned into a deep frown and Sia began to suspect that when Sebastian was quiet he was at his most dangerous.

'As in…'

'The most famous art forger in Europe? The man whose estimated profits were beyond ten million pounds? The man who was shopped to the police by his wife? *That* John Keating. Yes,' she replied, nodding. 'You see, I'm quite used to being in the company of infamy.'

As she said the words intended to bruise his ego a double-edged sword opened up a wound she'd thought had healed a while ago. Despite that, she pushed on. 'After my father's quite public arrest and the shocking scandal of my mother's betrayal, my Aunt Eleanor took me in. She is the opposite of her sister, Michaela. Conservative, steady job, never married—though I think taking care of me managed to scare away the few suitors who might have managed to get past her strong inclination towards disdain. But she took me in when she had very little money and no real obligation,' Sia concluded, still firm in the belief that she owed her aunt a great debt.

'She was your family, of course there was obligation,' Sebastian said, as if such a thing was as true to him as the sky was blue. But, for Sia, she wasn't so sure, because if it *were* true then her relationship with her mother might have been different.

'She put me in a good school and she gave me the boundaries that had been missing from my life with John and Michaela.'

'Where is your mother now?'

'Probably passed out in the bed of a married man.'

From the uncharacteristic look of shock on Sebastian's face, she could tell that her response had surprised him. But Sia had spent years compartmentalising her feelings about both her mother and her father, and it had been years since she'd actually seen her mother in person.

'Of all the careers you could have gone into, why art evaluation?'

'It's in my blood,' she answered immediately, as if there had never been any other option.

As Sebastian began to draw the information she had revealed together, painting his own picture of what it must have been like to try and pursue a career in a world where her name was not only infamous but linked to a man who had made it his life's work to deceive people like her future bosses… Not only was he incredibly impressed, he was also angry.

Angry because it wasn't supposed to have been Sia who had valued the painting. No, it should have been Sean Johnson, a man who *had* done enough to deserve whatever punishment Bonnaire's would lay upon Sia. Sebastian couldn't help but rub his jaw. Once again, the acrid taste of guilt on his tongue blotted out the heavy Bordeaux. He'd really messed things up for Sia Keating and presently he couldn't quite see a way for him to make it up to her without losing everything that he'd worked towards.

'Ask your question,' he stated.

'Why would Sheikh Abrani say that his painting was fake when it wasn't?'

INTERVIEWER ONE: *What kind of question is that?*

MS KEATING: *One he wasn't expecting.*

INTERVIEWER TWO: *Why didn't you just ask him where the painting was?*

MS KEATING: *He would have found a way round it.*

INTERVIEWER TWO: *But he promised to tell you the truth.*

MS KEATING: *[sighs] He would have said,* In a crate, *or* Somewhere safe, *or* I don't know—*which could easily have been the real answer if he'd asked someone to take it off his hands for a while and not tell him where it was being kept.*

INTERVIEWER TWO: *Huh.*

INTERVIEWER ONE: *So why did you ask about the Sheikh?*

It was honestly the very last thing that Sebastian had expected to come out of her mouth. He'd been curious to see what direction she would take and had certainly given her enough credit to know that she wouldn't be crass enough to come straight out and ask if he'd done it.

But that she'd veered so completely from what he'd expected, planned and prepared for her to ask… *That* was clever.

'I'm not sure how I would know the answer to that question,' he hedged.

'Take a run at it,' she said coolly, just as the wind picked up in the leaves on the plants placed at either corner of the roof terrace.

He looked across the skyline, unseeing of the shapes that interrupted the night sky, the way that lit windows merged with stars, the moon shining down on them all, and instead picked his words carefully.

'The Sheikh won't admit to the theft because it's in his interests also for there to be no fuss about this.'

'Why?'

'If there is a theft investigation then the police would be involved and they would discover that the Sheikh is hardly a pillar of the community.'

'But the theft has cost him one hundred million pounds,' Sia said, apparently appalled by the loss of an inconceivable sum of money.

'So, imagine the amount he's protecting from a criminal investigation. These days they're a little more hot on state representatives taking bribes and making backroom deals than they once were.'

'What do you mean?'

He sighed, not having imagined the turn the conversation would take that evening. 'What do you know of the Sheikh?' he asked.

'I met him only that once, when I was in Sharjarhere to evaluate the Durrántez.'

'What did you think of him?'

Sia searched her mind, unable to shake the feeling that this was some kind of test.

'I was only introduced to him and then he...' she shrugged '...left. I can't say that he filled me with warmth and joy, but he didn't have to.' Only that wasn't quite the truth. Now that she forced herself to look back and consider what he had been like, she remembered that she hadn't liked the way that he had treated his staff, nor the feeling that had permeated the walls of the palace. A feeling that was very much like fear, or the expectation of it at least.

'Let me tell you a little something about the Sheikh. Like many rulers, he is well educated, obscenely rich, incredibly well connected, which of course has absolutely nothing to do with the first two. On the surface he appears to be open-minded, fairly interested in ecological developments, was one of the first to sign the

Paris Climate Agreement, and has an incredible breeding programme for his thoroughbred racehorses which also seeks to support endangered animals.'

'What's not to like?' she asked, even though she knew that something was coming. Something she almost didn't want to know.

'What's not to like is that *beneath* the surface he is a despot who brings his full force down upon someone's head if he deems that person to have offended or simply not done as was asked. His vengeance is cruel, bordering on psychotic, and there are areas beneath his palace where family members are kept and abused for his pleasure. Their crime? Wanting to leave the country. Four of his daughters were married in political alliances before they were sixteen, and the youngest only managed to escape this fate by the fact he literally gambled away her hand in marriage. And that, Sia, was considered a *good* thing by his daughter. It was her only lifeline to freedom.'

'But that's...inconceivable.'

'Why, because you met him? You spent a few hours in his home? Because Bonnaire's would do business with him?'

'I can't believe it,' she said, even as his words were beginning to settle into a place that clicked with something already there in her mind.

'Sia, if you are so good at spotting fakes, look at me and tell me whether I'm lying.'

She didn't want to raise her eyes and meet his. Because she knew what she would find. And suddenly she was angry. Angry at Sebastian. If it hadn't been for him, she wouldn't have known about theft, forgery, nepotism, trapped family members, forced marriages and possible backroom deals at the company that employed her.

'You should go to bed. You've had a long day and will have another long day tomorrow.'

'Why?' she said, suddenly feeling the late hour of the evening against her skin.

'Because tomorrow we're going to the Caribbean.'

'What?'

'You don't have to come. But I'm keeping to my offer, for you to be my shadow for fourteen days. And my business doesn't stop for you, Ms Keating.'

'But I thought your business was doing as little as possible.'

'It is. I just like to be surrounded by exquisite beauty while doing it.'

How could he turn her feelings around with a carefully constructed and perfectly delivered line? Because whether *she* was the exquisite beauty he'd easily mentioned or the Caribbean, Sia couldn't say—not to mention her frustration at effectively being sent to bed. But she was beginning to see the pattern with Sebastian. He gave both truths and lies in equal measure so that she never knew where she stood with him.

Sebastian stayed outside for at least an hour after Sia departed. She might have been mad at him—it wasn't that hard to tell with her—but he'd had to send her away. He'd seen how the dawning realisation of what she'd got herself into had begun to chip away at her defences and he couldn't watch them crumble. She was going to need her armour—every inch of it— for what was coming. Because he simply could not afford to hold back.

CHAPTER FIVE

INTERVIEWER ONE: *So let me get this straight. The reason you didn't answer our calls was because you got on a plane with the man you believed to have stolen a painting from Bonnaire's and flew to the Caribbean?*

MS KEATING: *I believe he stole the painting from Sheikh Abrani—but yes.*

INTERVIEWER TWO: *Wouldn't you have?*

INTERVIEWER ONE: *[sotto] That's not the point.*

MS KEATING: *I thought it possible that the painting might be there.*

INTERVIEWER TWO: *And was it?*

WIND BUFFETED SIA'S hair, whipped at her thin long-sleeved T-shirt and almost managed to push her back an inch from where she stood beside the folded down steps to a private jet. But she braced herself against the wind, just as she ground her teeth together to prevent herself from slapping the smirk from Sebastian's handsome face.

The reason for the smirk was presently resting by his feet. The wooden crate, approximately twenty by twenty-four inches, also happened to be the exact measurements of the Durrántez painting *Woman in Love.*

'Are you sure you don't want to see inside of it?' he taunted.

'No, I'm fine, thanks.'

But she did. She *really* did. And he knew it. She couldn't work out whether he would be either that reckless or that arrogant to wave the real painting in front of her. But she would lose if she did look and lose if she didn't. At least by *not* doing so she could cling to the belief that it made her seem as if she didn't care.

Despite the traces of aviation fuel on the wind, there was something startlingly fresh about being in the middle of this flat, sparse private airfield outside of London. And Sia had to acknowledge that she felt much more awake and refreshed than she would have thought.

She'd imagined that in spending the night in Sebastian Rohan de Luen's townhouse she would have tossed and turned into the early hours, her mind whirling. But the moment her head had hit the pillow she'd fallen into a deep dreamless sleep. Before being woken up by Sebastian's servant. Or house man? She still didn't know what to call him.

All of which had meant that she hadn't spent the night wondering whether she should or shouldn't be going to the Caribbean with a suspected art thief, a confirmed international playboy. She'd been in too much of a daze to do anything other than agree when he'd first told her. And this morning?

If she said no she'd return to her flat in Archway, with no job for a month—and in all probability no pay either—and she'd be no closer to proving that she hadn't made a mistake. No. The only way she could ensure her professional reputation remained intact was to find the painting, and the only way she could do that was to follow him wherever he went.

She purposefully turned away from Sebastian, who was looking more attractive than anyone had a right to in a pair of aviation sunglasses, jeans that lovingly hugged his thighs and a dark blue long-sleeved Henley. Despite the casual look, everything exuded more money than she could earn in a month. She was on the verge of asking what they were waiting for when three dark, sleek town cars pulled onto the runway in an almost hypnotising procession.

They pulled up in a line beside the small jet and a man got out of the back of the middle car with a large black duffel bag handcuffed to each wrist. Sia watched, incredulous, as the man nodded to Sebastian, walked up the stairs, deposited the bags apparently in the back of the aeroplane and returned to the back of the middle town car, upon which all three of the sleek vehicles resumed their balletic procession and left the airfield.

'I don't believe you,' she tossed over her shoulder as she approached the stairs.

'What?' Sebastian asked, clearly finding it difficult to keep the laughter from his voice.

'You did that on purpose.'

'I don't know what you mean.'

'I don't think there's anything in those bags more important than kitty litter,' she ground out.

'To a cat owner without kitty litter they'd be pretty important,' he said, following her up the stairs and into the cabin.

As she poked her head into the surprisingly spacious area in the cabin and she rolled her eyes at the ridiculous duffel bags, each strangely strapped into a seat, her mobile phone vibrated in her pocket for the fourth time that morning.

'Please,' said Sebastian, 'don't let me stop you.'

'It's fine.'

'Are you sure? It could be important. And you won't be able to answer it in flight.'

She retrieved her phone and switched it off in front of him. But the problem was that she knew it probably was important. It had to be for Bonnaire's to have called her four times in the last hour and a half.

But they had suspended her. They had suspended her, and it didn't feel right. After the conversation with Sebastian the night before, she'd played the last meeting with her boss over and over again in her head. Why hadn't David been able to access her folders from the initial assessment? Why hadn't Abrani had the authentication papers to hand? He'd said he'd passed them onto Sean, but it was highly irregular to separate the papers from the painting. And she'd not seen them when she'd got back to Bonnaire's. And now she couldn't access the files to see if they had ever been there. But if they weren't, if they never had been... then Bonnaire's and Sean would have knowingly auctioned a painting without authentication papers, which was not exactly illegal. But the certificate of authentication acted like a sales receipt. It meant that they couldn't be sure that the Sheikh had come by the painting through legal means. And Bonnaire's shouldn't have been doing business under those circumstances. But they had.

'Please, sit where you like,' he said, cutting into her thoughts, before heading towards the cockpit.

She looked about her, trying to work out where she should sit. She waited for a moment for Sebastian to return from speaking to the pilot, but he didn't. Frowning, she gingerly made her way towards the cockpit and knocked on the door.

'Enter.'

'What do you think you're doing?' she demanded the moment she caught sight of him sitting in the pilot's seat.

'Flying us to the Caribbean,' he said with a smile that she was sure had dropped a few panties in its time.

'Ah...no. No, I don't think so.'

'You're more than welcome to follow on a commercial flight. I can have Benjamin book you a seat. You'll only be about fourteen hours behind me, but I'm sure you won't mind,' he taunted.

She was going to need a dentist by the time these fourteen days were up, she was clenching her jaw so much. She cast an eye across the vast number of little lights, some of which were flashing, some white, some red, all of which were too many for her to take in.

'I am a fully qualified pilot. We have blue skies, calm winds and should have a good flight time.'

The space was small, even with the two pilot

seats and…steering wheels, not that she thought they were actually called that.

'Sia.' His tone called her attention back to him. 'I can fly this plane. And I promise you, if you want to get the commercial flight—'

'No. No. I…ah…' she laughed a little '… I trust you. In *this* I trust you,' she said, realising that she did.

'I'm sorry.'

'Why?'

'That must have hurt.'

She couldn't help but slap him on the arm, an action that momentarily surprised them both.

'You're welcome to stay,' he said, levelling her with a gaze she felt to her toes.

She looked at the seat, trying to figure out how to even get into the thing, and realised that she'd already made the decision. There was a feeling of excitement edged with a little healthy fear and something not too far from adrenaline running through her veins as he helped her into the seat and the harness.

She watched, fascinated, as he spoke into the microphone attached to the earphones, communicating with whoever he needed to about taking off. The gentle forward movement as they began to head towards the runway seemed slower than a walk but, before she knew it, they were picking up speed and approaching the runway and she couldn't take the smile from her face, even if she couldn't loosen her grip on the arms of the seat. Sebastian took them faster and faster and never had she been more conscious that they were two little people inside a slightly bigger construction of metal and technology and, just when she would have shouted for him to stop, the wheels left the tarmac and they soared.

It took everything in her not to whoop, biting her lip, clenching her hands. None of it worked. When Sebastian looked across at her his smile, pantie-dropping or not, was one of pure joy.

What do you do for fun?

Let billionaire playboys fly me to the Caribbean.

Sebastian was still smiling as he pushed down the steps of his private jet and gestured for Sia to precede him. In truth, the flight had been much more enjoyable than expected, once Sia had relaxed. She'd refused his invitation to take the controls, but he suspected she might agree next time he offered. It'd been clear she had enjoyed it too.

Not that there would be a next time, he reminded himself firmly. They had thirteen days left and he couldn't lose sight of the threat that Sia posed for each and every one of those days as she pursued her investigation into the Durrántez painting. That alone meant he needed to keep her at arm's length.

But all of those thoughts disappeared as he caught sight of Ajay, his manager. He'd been looking forward to this moment for the last eighteen months and now the Caribbean hotel was on the verge of opening.

He had one duffel bag in each hand, which he unceremoniously threw into the back of the pick-up-style truck waiting beside the small sandy runway, before walking over to take the man in a strong embrace.

'It's good to see you,' Sebastian said sincerely, seeing the warm smile on his friend's face.

'And you, Sebastian. And you.'

'How are they?'

'The cabins are perfect and all finished, just in time.'

'Not the cabins, Ajay, your family,' Sebastian said, rolling his eyes.

'They're good too. Tia is teething, which is always fun.'

Sebastian turned to make an introduction, finding Sia looking at him with the ghost of a smile on her lips and intelligent assessment sparking in her eyes.

'Sia, allow me to introduce Ajay—a man without whom none of this would be here.' Ajay appeared embarrassed at the praise, but Sebastian had meant every word.

Sia stepped forward and greeted him warmly, 'It's lovely to meet you.'

'Likewise. However, I'm afraid that we do have a little business to touch on before you can relax until the party this evening.'

'There's going to be a party?' Sia asked him.

'Yes. It's…' Sebastian paused, choosing his words carefully, feeling that familiar sense of mischief he couldn't seem to stop around her. 'It's a pre-opening gala for VIPs,' he concluded, avoiding the confused look Ajay was giving him. 'Come on,' he said, opening the door to the Jeep for Sia. He was tempted to take the long way round, extending the short fifteen-minute drive to nearly twice that, but, checking his watch, realised they didn't have the time. Reluctantly, he pulled onto the main road—a laughable description of one of the only three roads on the island which he owned and where he'd decided to build his most recent hotel.

As the road drew closer to the shoreline, through the dense palms, flashes of azure-blue sea could be seen, golden sugary sand beckoned and sparks of fuchsia, purple and yellow from the exotic flowers exploded in his peripheral vision. In the mirror of the Jeep he caught Sia staring, her head turning from one side of the car to the other, eyes wide with wonder as the air through the open window played with the trails of her hair. He knew the feeling. He'd had that same sense of awe the first time he'd come here and knew that he had to have it.

The heat was bearable, having passed from the rainy season a few weeks before and, inhaling deeply, Sebastian felt a wave of relaxation pour over him in spite of the requirements for that evening. In too short a time they pulled up in front of the reception and Ajay jumped from the seat and was opening the door for Sia.

Sebastian had seen pictures of the reception

centre going up, and now that it was complete
he was impressed, but it was the centrepiece
inside he was desperate to see.

'Are they up?' he asked Ajay, who nodded,
his eyes shining with equal anticipation. 'How
do they look?' Sebastian couldn't help but ask.

'See for yourself.' Ajay gestured and Sebastian couldn't help but race up the stairs of the
only two-storey building on the whole island
so that he'd have just a few moments to himself to appreciate the dramatic impact of the
commissioned pieces before sharing them with
Ajay and Sia.

And those moments…they were needed because, as he inhaled with awe, he realised that
what Astou Ndiaye had created was nothing
short of incredible. Then he heard Sia's footsteps behind him and he turned to see her reaction.

Sia was speechless.

She'd followed Sebastian's swift departure
at a more sedate pace, instead taking in the
way that the building's thatch of rushes blended
beautifully with the palms and larger trees it
nestled within. Casting a quick glance further

down the stony road, she could see glimpses of entrances to equally discreet buildings in a similar style. And as she pushed open the cool glass door, frigid from the power of the interior air conditioning, she peered into the gloom and came to a sudden stop.

The reception area was spacious and reached up to the ceiling above the second-floor balcony wrapping around the open area. In the middle of the ground floor stood a beautiful dark wooden desk, polished to perfection. But that was not what Sia was staring at. Two breathtakingly large paintings hung either side of the desk, from the ceiling above the second storey all the way to the floor.

Each easily more than ten metres high and maybe seven or eight in width, the impact of the abstract paintings was both powerful and humbling. There was something almost baroque about them, Sia decided, like Poussin's mythological paintings—it was as if through the shapes and splatters, the drama of the paint Sia could almost see the mountainous pile of bodies from a war between angels and demons. Yet, within the heady mix of colour and texture, there were no figures, no humanity, just a broiling clash and energy that made her blood fizz as she was looking at them. As if they called her, challenged her to act, to reach, to want...

But, beneath all that, there was something niggling at her. Something vaguely familiar? She shook her head, unsettled by the feeling.

'You don't like them?' Sebastian asked.

'No, actually, I love them,' Sia replied. 'I just...can't place the artist.'

'Astou Ndiaye. She's Senegalese, living in France.'

'They are incredible pieces,' Sia concluded, realising that she'd neither heard of the artist nor remembered seeing a painting by her before.

'Yes, they are. A recent commission' Sebastian replied, not looking at the paintings but her. 'Bad news, I'm afraid,' he said, tucking something large under his arm, the action finally serving to tear her attention away from the paintings.

'Yes?'

'You're stuck with me. The accommodation is fully booked out for the VIP event this evening.'

'Wait…what?' she said, having to jog after him as he made his way out of the reception area and down a stone pathway overhung by large green leafy palms, so thick they almost blocked out the sun's rays.

'It's just that the accommodation was arranged a month ago. I had hoped that there may have been a cancellation, but it seems tonight my hotel is *the* place to be.' Despite the fact that Sebastian was walking ahead of her, Sia was sure that she could hear a tone to his voice. A sarcastic one. 'But we're both adults,' he continued, 'and I'm sure we'll cope.'

'Cope with what?' she asked as they rounded a corner, Sia having to duck out of the way of a palm she suspected he had swung her way on purpose.

'One bed.'

'What?' Sia demanded and had to pull up short to prevent herself from marching straight into the back of Sebastian.

He turned, grinned at her and announced, 'Here we are,' with a shrug and walked straight up the stairs of the most incredible 'cabin' she'd ever seen. 'Are you coming?' he asked, standing at the top of the short steps that led up to decking wrapping around an open-fronted Caribbean bungalow.

This playful Sebastian was new… Not new as such, just carefree rather than taunting. Or at least that was how he seemed. Her feet dragged unaccountably as she followed him up the steps, until she turned to look out at the view and, once again, Sia was speechless. In front of her lay a crescent-shaped bay, sweeping around to her right. On one side of the decking was a small, square but surprisingly deep pool that looked as if it merged with the sea on the horizon. On the other side was a hammock stretching lazily from beneath the thatched awning to a post at the far corner of the decking.

The riot of colours that greeted her were so intense and overwhelming she had to remind herself to breathe. She huffed out a laugh. Only three days ago she had been at her desk in her one-bedroom flat in Archway, peering through the gloom, desperately trying to find the man who had caused her to be suspended from work. The same man who had flown her halfway round the world, *himself*, and was sharing his accommodation with her.

'Do you like it?' she heard from behind her.

And perhaps it was because she hadn't seen him, wasn't distracted by his mask, that she could sense the underlying plea in his tone. He wanted her to like it. And she couldn't bring herself to lie.

'Yes. Very much,' she said, turning to find him standing much closer than she'd expected.

'Good,' he said, only it came out as a whisper that she felt against her lips, lips that she instantly bit down upon to stop the tingling from spreading.

Looking past him, she couldn't help but be drawn into the cabin. Large beautiful wooden ceiling fans hung low and swung silently, creating a gentle but welcome breeze. A huge bed dominated the space, surrounded by mosquito netting that looked more pretty than functional. To the left, out in the open, was a claw-foot white enamel high-backed bath facing out to the view behind her.

'It is a couple's cabin,' Sebastian explained. 'The toilet facilities are in the only room with a door, behind the bed.'

Sia picked up the brochure from a wooden table with gold inlay and eyed the condensation-covered ice bucket and its bottle of champagne

warily. But not as warily as the pair of binoculars also on the table.

'Bird-watching?' she asked, her tongue working around the double entendre.

'As you can see, there is no direct view into
anyone else's cabin, so it really is for the wild-
life.'

She walked towards the large, dark wooden
object that he'd carried with him from reception.

'And this is…?'

'A screen. You will want to bath and to dress.'
Her raised eyebrow seemed to bruise his ego.
'I'm a playboy, not a monster.'

'Duly noted,' she said, unfolding the intri-
cately carved wooden teak screen. It was a mar-
vel of artistry, much like the entire hotel. She
was focusing on the small details because it
helped. Helped her to ignore the current spinning beneath her skin at a rate of knots. The
entire cabin, aside from the toilet, was open-
plan and, as much as she tried not to, her eyes
kept returning to the impossibly large bed.

'I'll be sleeping on the hammock. Outside,'
he added.

Sia turned and hid the slight tinge of disappointment beneath a smile.

'But your dress won't arrive for another hour, so—'

'Dress?'

'I wasn't sure that you had packed one, so I took the liberty.'

That he was right didn't make him any more…any more…right. And she hated that he was right.

'So,' he continued, 'I'm going to get washed and changed.'

He was looking at her and seemed to be waiting for something but… 'Oh. Of course. I'll be outside,' she said awkwardly when she realised he was waiting for her to leave.

Shaking her head, hoping that it wasn't a smile she saw across Sebastian's face from the corner of her eye, she made her way out to the decking, her back firmly against the wall of the cabin. She exhaled a shaky laugh at her own foolishness and locked her gaze on the stunning horizon, purposely focusing on the feeling of excitement fizzing through her veins and not the aching thrill she was beginning to get whenever she looked at Sebastian.

She wanted to take this all in. She might have been to some far-flung and incredible places but each and every one of them was for work. Holidays with Aunt Eleanor had been to caravan parks at the end of long drives. Lovely, but very English—sunburnt moss and grass verges, sandy dunes that tipped down into a cool grey sea. This, the Caribbean, was almost the opposite. Everything seemed electric, even the colours, and Sia found it strangely stimulating rather than relaxing.

Being here was so completely different to her life in London, her one-bedroom flat and her almost constant working hours. Or, rather, what she'd *made* of her life in London? She had gone from university to the only place that had offered her a job and her gratitude had bordered on desperate, taking whatever valuation they'd given her, going wherever they told her to, working whatever hours they'd needed. All those things? That had been on her. The shape of the hole she'd forced herself into was one of *her* design. Perhaps, when all this was done, she should think about that design a little more. Maybe it wasn't the right fit any more.

Breathing past the dull ache in her chest, she

looked up to find the most beautiful bird soaring through the sky. She turned to ask Sebastian what it might be, when her eyes took in the sliver of space between the wooden screen and the mirror behind the bath.

Words screeched to a halt on her tongue as her eyes clung to the taut muscles of his shoulders and neck as he angled his head further back to make room for the razor he was drawing delicately beneath his jaw.

Shirtless, his trousers hanging low, the top button undone, leaving the corners of his waistband open like a book, the contours of his abdomen were almost perfection. Side on, she could see the groove running from his hipbone to deep beneath the waist of his trousers.

All she wanted to do was run her fingers over his skin, to outline the rise and fall of his muscles, to feel the warmth of his body, not smooth and cold like marble, but warm and rough and real. There was a breadth and a power to him that he concealed beneath expensive suits and pithy remarks. There was something thin about the impression that gave—insubstantial. But here, now... Sia had to plant her feet on the decking to stop herself from walking forward.

There was strength and a sense of something immoveable. Something thrilling. Her body began to heat from deep within, radiating outward in pulses that made her want to clench her thighs together. And suddenly all she wanted was to be the focus of all that strength and power. He angled his head to the other side, and she watched as he drew the razor from his throat upwards and she could no longer hide from the pure desire coursing through her veins.

Sebastian felt it. The moment her gaze struck his skin. It had been a spark that jolted his heart, his pulse and his arousal at the same time. For just a second his hand shook, he nearly nicked his jaw but pulled away just in time. He took a deep breath and relished it, inhaled the electricity he could feel. He was hyperaware of every movement, conscious of every turn of his head, almost every hair the razor's edge covered.

He delayed it until he couldn't resist any longer. He wanted to see her, wanted to glean something, anything, in her reaction in that moment. Was she aroused like him? Did she feel every inch of her skin and senses? She *had* to, surely. Only mutual attraction burned this brightly.

The moment his eyes met hers in the mirror he was very glad he'd put his razor down. It had been like a tsunami, one giant wave crashing over him and drawing him under, pounding against him with shocking force, all of which suddenly disappeared the moment she dropped her gaze.

He was playing with fire and he knew it.

It took him the next twenty minutes to get himself under control. By which time he was ready and the package from Reception had arrived.

He stepped out onto the decking to find her looking out at the horizon again.

'Your turn,' he said and at first he thought it funny the way she avoided his gaze. Until he realised that it was most definitely not. Because, this close up, he could see that it wasn't the act of an experienced tease, it wasn't a play at being coquettish.

That was innocence. Pure and true. And he felt it like a slap to the face. Tangling with the enemy was one thing, but that? Not his style. He preferred women who knew the score, a few nights of incredible pleasure...but after? A very happy and equally willing *adios*. Easy, enjoyable but, most importantly, short and simple.

And there was nothing simple about Sia and nothing short about what he wanted to do with her. So he ignored the urge to turn and discover whether she had closed the gap in the wooden screen or left it open for him, the thought firing his blood and his determination to leave Sia Keating the hell alone.

What felt like only seconds later, the sound of heels on the wooden decking drew him round and he had to bite his tongue to stop himself from heaping praise on her. From head to toe she was exquisite. He'd chosen the dress knowing that it was different to her usual style, but she looked... *Like everything he'd ever wanted.*

He shook the thought from his head and instead said a different truth. 'You should always dress like this.'

It was turquoise in colour, thin shoulder straps led to a V that hugged her breasts and dropped into a beaded bodice that was reminiscent of art deco in design. Flashes of turquoise-coloured square sequins flashed in the setting sun, nestled next to gold sequins so pale they matched Sia's skin, giving the impression of bare skin. Waterfalls of silk fell from her waist which swayed with each step she took towards him.

He could have bitten off his own tongue. He never should have bought this dress for her.

'It's hardly suitable for the office. It's very beautiful *and* generous, but I'm not sure it's me,' she said, fanning out the skirts around her legs.

'It is bold, courageous and sensual, which makes me wonder if it's the office that doesn't suit? It certainly reminds me of the woman I met in Victoriana,' he said truthfully.

'That wasn't me.'

'Are you sure about that?'

'Absolutely.'

'Well, that is a shame. Because *Henri* was impressive, passionate and powerful. Who stole that from you, Sia?' he couldn't help but ask.

'The deal is that *I* ask *you* the question. We had no agreement on me answering yours.'

He could see that she was hurt and angry. He knew that he'd pushed a button, but her retaliation was swift, harsh and, once again, it caught him unprepared.

'So, tell me what you see when you look at the Durrántez painting,' she demanded.

'My mother.'

Both the speed and his answer seemed to surprise them both.

'Literally or figuratively?'

He breathed in, needing a moment to secure a smile full of charm across his lips. 'One question per day, Sia. You know that.'

CHAPTER SIX

INTERVIEWER ONE: *What was this gala? I don't remember seeing anything in the newspapers.*

INTERVIEWER TWO: *You said it was for VIPs?*

MS KEATING: *Yes, it was. Very important people.*

SIA TRIED TO shake off the mess of her thoughts as she followed Sebastian back towards the hotel reception on the high-heeled shoes he'd somehow managed to secure *in the right size*. In part she'd brought it on herself. Her question had been born of her own hurt, her own frustration that Sebastian saw something in her that she'd never seen in herself but wanted to. Had *always* wanted to. But she'd also wanted to know why the Durrántez was so important to him and his answer had only confused her.

A confusion that swirled around her like the

skirts of the most beautiful dress she'd ever worn. But, no matter how wonderful it made her feel, how…sensual and bold—just as he'd said—she still didn't feel as if it suited her. Henri, perhaps. But not Sia, Bonnaire's art valuer. If she would ever be that again. *If she even wanted to be.*

She matched Sebastian's pace as it slowed to a stop, where he greeted some guests also making their way to the reception area. She didn't recognise the faces of the people that passed, but everyone was smiling and happy. She felt Sebastian's arm at her back as he guided her up the steps beside him and through the doorway.

The reception area had completely changed in the last few hours. Strings of fairy lights led from above the entrance to the opposite side of the room, as if guiding the guests towards the beautiful terrace area beyond. Unable to resist, Sia followed the others towards the steps out onto a back garden area that she had missed on their first visit.

Even more lights hung in a canopy above the garden and it was as if the stars had come closer just for them. Large broad-leafed palms interspersed with purple allamanda and jasmine created a beautiful, scented border for the party. Waiters in loose linen uniforms slowly circled the guests, offering flutes of champagne, pitchers of fresh fruit juice and platters of delicious-looking canapés.

And as she looked about her, Sia realised that, although everyone was dressed in finery, it wasn't the kind of obscene wealth she'd have imagined of a highly exclusive private event on a Caribbean island. One strange difference was that the guests genuinely seemed to be happy to be there, as if they actually knew each other rather than being there simply to be seen before finding somewhere else more important to be.

'Sia, you look beautiful,' Ajay said sincerely by way of introduction.

'Thank you.'

'I don't think she likes it,' Sebastian stage-whispered to his hotel manager, seeming to return to the funny self-deprecating figure he tended to become around Ajay, as if the awkwardness they had shared had disappeared like clouds on a summer's day.

'I do,' Sia said immediately, not wanting to seem ungrateful, but couldn't help feeling self-conscious as Sebastian once again seemed to gaze at her from head to toe before turning back to Ajay.

'Is it time?'

'Yes, sir.'

With a smile flashed in her direction, Sebastian left them and headed towards the decking area, stopping at the top of the stairs and waiting until everyone naturally grew silent.

'There is one thing that I like to do before the opening of every one of my hotels. It started with my first and has continued on from there. I like to bring *the* most important people together. You,' he said, offering his hands to the guests, and as she looked around the beaming faces she saw more than just happiness. She saw pride.

'You have worked beside me on this endeavour—contractors, suppliers, staff. This night is to say a huge and deeply heartfelt thank you for everything that you have done and have achieved. Tonight, I have brought in staff from other hotels around the world, not only to serve you, but for them to see what incredible things you've done. Tonight, you are the guests, the *first* guests of this hotel. So eat, drink, enjoy the cabins and the entertainment. I don't want to see any of you before at least midday tomorrow!'

A huge round of applause, a wave of laughter and a cheer rippled out across the small crowd, but Sia only had eyes for Sebastian. *The most important people, indeed.* Ajay cast her a knowing smile and led her to where delicious plates of food were being served while Sebastian stopped to shake hands and give thanks to some of the guests.

As Sebastian looked around he felt pleasure in their success, a thrill in seeing all the changes to the designs he'd made to ensure the buildings worked harmoniously with the backdrop. He remembered wrestling with the first architect—a very intelligent and experienced man, but his heart had been in chrome and steel, not in working sympathetically with the setting, local materials or even local experts. When Ajay had introduced his cousin, Sebastian knew he'd found the right man for the job.

The hotel had been done right and perfectly. But—Sebastian managed to stop himself from shaking his head—he thought he'd feel more... Just *more.* Here he was, with everything he'd ever wanted. Revenge had been taken against the Sheikh, his sister was happily married with a child on the way. His father and Valeria were safely in Rimini doing their own thing. But from the age of eighteen he'd done everything he *had* to. Then, in the last three or so years, anything he *could* do. But as he looked out to where the sea stretched beneath the stars, dark shapes twisting in the moonlight, he couldn't help but wonder if this was what he really *wanted* to do.

Instinctively, he was drawn back to the gathering, the cascade of laughter he recognised as Sia's and was suddenly, and completely irrationally, jealous of Ajay, who was a very happily married man and father of two.

She would make an incredible mother.

The thought popped into his head and caught there. He could see it in his mind's eye—her gently casting circles over a baby bump, a little more pink to her cheeks, the beautiful red-gold hair flowing down her back. The image was so pure, so true, it was as if he knew it was in her future—something she not only wanted but deserved. But, just as strongly, Sebastian knew it would not be in his. He'd experienced that heavy weight of responsibility, knew what it took to protect and safeguard that family and three years ago had decided he was done.

At eighteen, he'd been a teenager who'd sold his family belongings to keep the roof over his and his sister's heads. While his father and Valeria had sailed around Greece for months on end, Sebastian had gone to school plays, parent teacher conferences and spent every spare minute ensuring his first hotel was a success. And then the second. And the third. In the first five years of their exile he'd barely slept more than four hours a night. And not just because of the fact he worked all the hours God sent, but because of the fear. The fear that it could all be taken away again in the blink of an eye. The fear that nothing in this world was really lasting.

The sound of a glass breaking drew him back to the present, as highly efficient staff descended to resolve the situation. His mind refocused and he looked back to where Sia stood, taking a canapé from a silver tray on the table at the side and smiling up at Ajay with pure joy. No pregnancy bump, no thoughts of future family or responsibilities.

There was only now, only this moment and Sebastian couldn't resist the urge to show her just how much fun that could be.

'I hope you didn't mind Sebastian's joke,' Ajay said, pouring a little more champagne into her glass.

'I don't think it *was* a joke. These clearly are very important people to the hotel and to the island,' she said with a smile, unable to stop herself from swaying to the beat of a song played by an unobtrusive DJ. Because that was the thing about Sebastian—he seemed to play on expectations, both living up to and undercutting them at any given moment so that she never really knew where she stood with him. Never know what was real and what was not. She'd told him that she was good at spotting fakes, but she was beginning to doubt it when it came to him.

'We were so thankful to hear that Mr Rohan de Luen had closed the deal on the island. The first prospective buyer had plans to develop almost every inch of it. Our island isn't as big as some of the others, so the sale could have meant the loss of jobs as well as housing. But Sebastian found a way to make it work for all of us.'

'I'm surprised. For someone who generally seems very happy to brag, he's been particularly tight-lipped about all this,' she said, casting an eye over the large courtyard.

'Men don't brag about what's important to them,' Ajay leaned into confide.

'Which is why you'll never hear about his incredibly beautiful wife and two delightfully perfect daughters,' Sebastian leaned in to interrupt. 'May I?'

He held his hand out to Sia and she was genuinely concerned he was asking her to dance.

'I don't—'

'No one will start until I do and I'm not dancing with Ajay.'

'Yes, but I *can't*.'

'I don't believe that for a second. When was the last time you danced?'

'When I was seven?'

'Well, that's just plain stupid.'

'Stupid?' she asked, half laughing. 'You are trying to get me to dance with you by calling me stupid?'

'Is it working?' he asked, charm sparkling in

his eyes and a smile that was horrifyingly ir-resistible. 'Please?'

She'd have liked to blame it on the gentle buzz in her veins from the two glasses of cham-pagne, or the way the natural heat from the Caribbean had already sunk into her body, eas-ing what felt like years of tension, but as she placed her hand in his, allowed him to lead her to a small flat area squared above by large bright bulbs, she knew it wasn't any of those things.

'You've been swaying to the beat of the last two songs, so I know you have rhythm,' he said, looking at her in a way that she turned away from. A blush rose to her cheeks at the thought he'd been watching her for that long. 'But if you're happy for me to take the lead?'

Sia nodded, incapable of untangling her tongue long enough to respond. And then she wished she'd refused, as he swept his arm around her waist and drew her into the warmth of his body. With barely an inch of space be-tween her chest and his, his thighs brush-ing against the skirts of her dress, moulding them between her legs, he guided her around the space. She felt it, that need welling within her, pulsing within her chest, creeping up to her throat as if desperate to...to...she honestly couldn't tell. Sebastian's hand flexed against the base of her spine as if he were struggling with the same thing—a build-up of electricity that needed to be released.

She let him move her body around the dance floor and she felt as if she were floating, light as a feather, completely at his mercy and it was wondrous. His grip was secure but not tight, powerful yet restrained, and she wanted more. His steps began to slow and she couldn't resist looking up at him as he looked down at her, the gentle puff of his breath on her lips, the way that his gold-flecked irises retracted to make space for enlarged pupils, his arm around her waist drew her against him just that bit closer and her heart felt as if it might explode. She wanted him to kiss her. So much it hurt. It actually hurt.

And just when she thought he might, just when he'd begun to close the distance between their lips, he paused...

And a round of applause exploded around them like gunfire, shredding the moment just as effectively.

Sia bit her lip against the seesawing of her emotions and thoughts. After all, he had told her his purpose was to gather other guests to dance and she managed a smile at the couples now filling the dance area. So anything she'd thought might have been about to happen? Just in her imagination.

Smiling gamely, she called to Ajay and asked him to dance. Thankfully, the music was much more upbeat and the fun, simple twirls he guided Sia into were easier to manage. Every now and then she'd catch a glimpse of Sebastian at the side of the dance floor, her eyes drawn to him by the feeling of his gaze tracking her every move, but each time she raised her face to his he was facing the person he was talking to. So she cast off the feeling and instead focused on determinedly enjoying herself.

He'd held her in his arms and he shouldn't have. Because now he knew what that felt like he'd never forget it as long as he lived. It was like holding a live wire. Exhilarating, terrifying, humbling and addictive. She'd been avoiding him ever since the end of the first dance and he knew why. It was much safer for her to think that it had all been for show. It hadn't, of course. But safer for her to believe that.

Because he was almost one hundred per cent sure that if he got one taste of her it would most definitely not be enough. Gritting his jaw, he told himself firmly that Sia Keating would remain untouched for the next twelve days before he sent her on her way. Perhaps with a quiet word in the ears of a few well-placed people in the art industry. She needed to get away from Bonnaire's and their sullied reputation.

Ajay was leading a smiling and seemingly happy Sia from the dance area back towards him. He wished he had a camera in that moment. She looked younger, the flush on her cheeks healthy and the shine in her eyes? Just incredible.

'I declare the evening a roaring success,' Sebastian said with a tilt of his champagne glass in Ajay's direction.

'Yes. The staff—'

'Guests.'

'The *guests* will remember this for a long time, Sebastian. It was a good idea.'

'I think we should do it once a year, not just for the opening,' Sebastian said, feeling the rightness of it the moment the words were out of his mouth.

'For Christmas?' Sia asked.

'It's a big season for us,' Ajay replied, unsure.

'March is fairly quiet. And we could get staff from other hotels to cover and, in return, we cover them, which would also allow staff to see how other hotels around the world are run.'

'See?' Ajay said, smiling, bumping his shoulder against Sia's and once again accidentally twisting a knife in Sebastian. 'He says "we".'

Sia nodded knowingly and Sebastian couldn't tell whether he was happy or irritated that they had been talking about him.

There were still a few guests dancing and milling around, but Sebastian was eager to go. He told himself he wanted to find a moment of quiet, away from the music and the hum of conversation around him, but he knew that wasn't true.

After a few more goodbyes than he'd intended, Sebastian led Sia back to the path away from the guests still partying. It was dark but the walkway's pale stones shone in the moonlight, leading them safely back to the cabin.

He ducked under low-hanging palm leaves and held them out of the way for Sia. But when he didn't feel her following he turned to find her looking up at the stars, wonder on her face, lost in a private moment he didn't want to disturb.

'It's almost otherworldly, isn't it?' she asked, surprising him.

Casting a look up to the velvet sky, the bright stars nestled in the smoky swirl of cosmos, 'Very different to London?' he couldn't help but ask.

'Just a tad.'

'Where in London do you live?' He had been honest with her when he'd said he'd not looked into her or her background. It was almost novel—learning about someone only by what they said and by what he trusted.

'North. Archway. It's handy for work.'

'But?' he asked, sensing some hesitancy there.

'I'm a South London girl at heart,' she said, finally turning her face from the heavens to his, grinning with a strange kind of home town pride. 'I grew up in Peckham with Mum and Dad and then later, just up the road in Forest Hill with Aunt Eleanor.'

'Why did you have to live with your aunt? Wasn't it only your father who was arrested?'

'It was decided that it would be better for me to live with her.'

'Decided by who?' He hadn't missed either the pause or the clipped tone to her voice, but couldn't help but ask.

'Everyone.'

'Including you?' he asked, incredulous, thinking if he could have just one minute, thirty seconds, ten, five even with his mother again he'd sell his soul for them. He'd come to a stop while she'd continued walking and she was now ahead of him. Even so, he didn't miss the sound of breath puffed between her lips.

'Yes. Mum is a complicated person.'

'But—'

She turned on him then, spinning round as if all the pent-up frustration and hurt that he'd missed in her tone was finally escaping.

'I get my hair from *her*,' Sia practically spat, hating the bitterness in her own voice but unable to stop. 'I got my name from my dad, but my hair from her. I don't look like her in any other way. Nose, eyes, face shape...' she gestured to herself '...that's the Keating side. But the hair?' She huffed out a bitter half laugh. 'She always said that she gave me the one thing that made me stand out.' As Sia spoke the words a childhood hurt rose up within her. That horrible scarring feeling that she wasn't enough on her own, in her own right, that everything she had was dependent on and because of her mother. She couldn't see past the memories and thoughts to find Sebastian. She was lost to it now. 'I tried to dye it once. Brown. It didn't work that well,' she said flippantly of one of the most excruciating moments of her teenage years. 'It turned into this kind of sludgy, streaked mess. I thought Mum would lose her mind. But she didn't even notice.

'There was quite a lot my mother didn't notice when I lived with them,' she pressed on, unable to stop now. 'Bedtime, I could stay up as long as I liked. Mealtimes, whenever and whatever I wanted, as long as I could get it for myself. School was an if and when thing,' she said, shrugging, 'which for my mother was very little of the "when". I learned my trade at my father's feet. Even at the age of seven I did a mean Pollock,' she said honestly and bitterly.

'And Mum had one focus in life—Dad. She

loved him. She loved him more than anything else in this world. She saw only him. And when he didn't see her, when he would spend weeks lost in front of his canvases, locked in the studio day and night... It hurt her. Broke her. Initially she would rage. Throw anything she could get her hands on—glasses, plates... There was a particularly close call with a kitchen knife once,' she said with a wobbly laugh as if it had been humorous rather than terrifying. 'Oh, the things she would scream at him.'

You're a photocopier! Good for nothing but copying.

You're not even an artist. Piss artist, more like.

Sia shivered at the memory, the shrieking South London accent cutting through the beautiful warmth of the Caribbean and reminding her where she came from. She felt the sheen of tears in her eyes covering a pain so close to the surface, like the shimmer on an over-inflated balloon, and she vaguely wondered if it was about to burst. Perhaps it already had and she just hadn't noticed.

'The neighbours called the police one too many times and she spent a few weeks in prison. Dad barely noticed, but he was there to pick her up. After that, she tried a different tack. She thought she could make John Keating jealous,' Sia scoffed. 'There was this party, very bohemian. Mum had draped silks over cheap lamps, candles everywhere. It was a miracle the place didn't burn down. She was all over the shop, flirting desperately with men, trying to provoke some kind—any kind—of reaction from my dad. And the most painful thing about it all was that I could see, *everyone* could see, that he just didn't care. He didn't laugh, he didn't get angry. He may as well have just told the men that they could have her,' she said, pressing her lips together against the hurt cry of her childhood wanting to get out.

'You asked me who stole my passion?' she said, finally turning to Sebastian, seeing him in the present and not hidden by the past. '*She* did. My mother. She taught me that passion was selfish, cruel, mean and hysterical and, in the end, utterly pointless. So forgive me if I don't live like you. *Love* like you. It's because even if I took the risk to, the fact that I could end up even remotely like her? Not worth it. Ever.'

She turned round and would have stalked off

had Sebastian not slipped his arm around her waist and held her against him to prevent her from leaving.

'That wasn't passion, Sia. What your mother felt, what motivated her actions…it wasn't passion,' he said gently, as if trying to soothe her, unconsciously evoking the very thing they were talking about and the last thing she wanted.

'Please…' she begged, hoping that he would stop, wanting him to continue, to say something that would lessen the pain of her heart breaking—for the past and the present.

She heard him sigh as if he'd lost some internal battle. Felt his head bend, as if in defeat, to rest on her shoulder, leaning ever so slightly into the crook of her neck.

'The Latin origin of passion…it means to suffer. To endure. Passion is a suffering that you take on yourself for what you want. It has nothing to do with inflicting that suffering on another.'

And then he let her go.

CHAPTER SEVEN

SEBASTIAN PUSHED OFF the wooden post with his foot, sending the hammock gently swaying beneath a spangled night sky, and cursed himself. He wasn't quite sure what for, only that he knew he deserved it.

The full moon was so large and so bright it could have passed for that hour just before dawn, but at the last check of his watch it was barely one-thirty. With everything half lit, it felt half real… *A time for fairies and magic,* his mother would have whispered in his ear and he smiled sadly at the memory.

With one arm behind his head and the other hanging lazily down to where the ice-cold bottle of beer he'd retrieved from the outside fridge sat gathering condensation from the heat of the night, his eyes watched the sky, his mind skipping over the possibilities and infinities of the world. His lips curved into a half smile as he saw the bright burn and tail of a shooting star slash across the darkness as his unconscious mind made a wish he was barely aware of. Shaking off the abstract thought of Sia as more of a want than a wish, impossible either way, he pushed off against the post again.

He should never have extended this offer of fourteen days. He should never have allowed himself to get so distracted. He didn't care about himself but the others, they had so much more to lose and he would never put them in danger like that. Yes, they'd all agreed, but still. It had been his plan, his idea…and he'd been the one to push it. Sia was a threat to all of that. He thought of Sia's question earlier about what he saw when he looked at the painting. And then Sia's answer when he'd asked who'd stolen her passion. He shook his head. Strange that they had both fought the same demons for incredibly different reasons.

He was about to snag hold of his beer when a creak on the decking stopped the movement. Every inch of him surged, the hairs on his arms lifted, he swore he could hear the thud of his heart, the rush of blood in his veins.

'Go to bed.'

The command was gravelly and low even to

his own ears. His eyes firmly on the horizon at sea, he knew, *knew*, that if he turned, if he caught sight of her there would be no going back.

'No.'

'You don't want this,' he warned.

'Who are you to tell me what I want and don't want? A thief? A liar?' Her words struck him like bullets.

'I have never lied to you.'

'Then tell me you're not attracted to me.'

He clamped his jaw shut but it did nothing to prevent the growl in his throat. Carefully and deliberately, he placed one foot and then the other on the decking and turned himself out of the hammock, his eyes neither on her or the horizon but somewhere in between. As if holding off the inevitable for as long as possible.

Finally, he faced her and he swallowed the curse on his tongue. The Prussian-blue silk negligée hung from thin shoulder straps, dipping in a Vee into a diamond panel that hugged her stomach beneath breasts so perfect his mouth watered. The bias cut ensured that the silk, shimmering beneath the moonlight, skated over the dips and swells of her hips and thighs, dusky shadows hinting at the secrets of her body. Long locks of rich auburn hair fell against the deep blue of the negligée, making her look more regal than any queen. But the look in her eyes as she took him in, running over his shirtless torso and snagging on the trousers hanging low on his waist, her pupils wide and shining in the moonlight...*that* was what nearly undid him. He fisted his hands at his sides and then forced them open.

'I'm not a Neanderthal,' he said, although it was quite possibly the first lie he'd told her. 'I can be attracted to a woman and not act on it, for God's sake.'

Sia was confused, hurt and more than a little frustrated. He'd made her want. He'd made her confront her feelings, her desire for him. And it was overwhelming and she ached. For him but just as much for herself. She *wanted* to be the passionate, bold person he had met at Victoriana, the woman who drank with billionaires, wore turquoise dresses, danced and laughed. But, more than that, she wanted to be the person who reached for what she wanted, for what she knew was right. But now he was refusing to let her. The playboy who had whatever he wanted, whenever he wanted, didn't want her?

'Why would you do this?' She couldn't help the tremor in her tone.

'I didn't do it for me, Sia. I did it for you,' he said, easing a hand over his face as if frustrated. 'So that you realise that it's okay to be a passionate, vibrant woman who owns not only her desires but has the courage to act on them *safely*.'

'And you're not safe?'

'Not to you.'

All this time she'd thought of passion as chaotic, scary, unbalanced, but that was because of what her mother had experienced, how her mother had behaved—selfish and needy, it had all been about her. But also, Sia believed, because it had been one-sided. Her father hadn't loved her mother and it had made her crazy.

Sebastian *was* attracted to her, and she wanted to know what that was like, what it *felt* like. Because suddenly it seemed as if it would be something beautiful, as if it would be the coming together of two halves of a whole. What had he said? He didn't have to act on it.

Perhaps they didn't, but she wanted so much just to allow herself to feel it.

'Would you...' she said, struggling to find the words to ask for what she wanted. 'Would you just stand here with me? No words. Just for a minute. I... I just want to know what it feels like.'

She thought she'd have to explain what she meant, but understanding shifted across his features and after a moment he nodded. She walked out onto the decking to meet him, not breaking the connection of his gaze. He watched her as if both wary and wanting.

She came to a stop a few inches from him, the distance greater than when they had danced together and yet so much more intimate. She tried to tell herself his body was nothing she hadn't seen before, in paintings, statues, pictures and even in person from the opposite side of the room. But being so close to Sebastian, his bare chest a study in perfection, was altogether completely different. Her pulse beat erratically and she inhaled slowly and deeply, attempting to soothe it.

She glanced at Sebastian, expecting to see a knowing, taunting gaze in his eyes but no, that wasn't what she found. Instead, he seemed to be watching everything about her, taking in as much as possible in exactly the same way as she had been and there was nothing remotely humorous in his gaze. When his eyes joined hers there was such a serious intensity there, something beyond words, beyond explanation or justification. She felt it in every single inch of her body, this strange sense of being known, seen.

And then, in a heartbeat, it changed.

It was as if a flame had been lit beneath their feet, licking up their flesh in an undulating tide, utterly overwhelming and urgent, demanding and angry almost. This time, when she caught his eyes, all she could feel was the power of just how much he wanted her and how much he fought it and it was incredible to behold.

She felt it, the moment he wanted to break the connection, the second before he would turn away.

'If I sleep with you, do you expect me *not* to go to the police about the painting?' she blurted out.

'What?' Sebastian replied, clearly confused

at the turn of the conversation. 'Of course not!' he said, as if outraged by the suggestion.

'If I sleep with you, will you ignore my wishes, my words, if I say stop—?'

'Sia, no. There will be no—'

'If I sleep with you—'

'This is not a game Sia. This is—'

'My choice, is it not?' She paused, waiting for him to interrupt. When he didn't she pressed on, her breath high with hope in her lungs, 'If I say stop?'

'Of course I would stop,' he said shortly.

'So why won't you start?' she asked, trying to keep the desperation out of her tone.

'Because you're innocent, Sia. You don't know what it is you're asking.'

'Don't patronise me,' she replied and this time *she* was frustrated.

'I'm not,' he said sincerely. 'No one does. You don't know what emotions this will bring, how you will feel in the morning. Better for it to be with someone who is in your life for the right reasons and for the long haul. Not...'

'Someone who has lost me my job and, in less than twelve days now, will leave and not look back? I know the deal, Sebastian,' she said, just as sincerely.

But she began to feel a little like her mother. As if she were desperate, dependent on him even. On the verge of begging, she hauled herself back from the brink. She wouldn't do that to herself, no matter how much she wanted Sebastian.

And that was when she realised that she wasn't like her mother at all and the release of the chains she hadn't realised were holding her back was so great that she felt as if she were soaring free. The light welling up within her, the power of it... She took a deep breath, allowing it to fill her completely, and she shook her head in wonder. Had her fear been holding her back all this time? Was this what she could have felt like—this powerful, this free all this time? Rather than feeling the loss, she marvelled at it and knew that she had Sebastian to thank. But in spite of that she also knew what she had to say, what she *wanted* to say.

'Despite what you think, I *do* know what I want. But I won't be like her. I won't beg and I won't be desperate.'

She turned to leave when his hand caught her wrist and spun her back round to face him.

'You're nothing like her,' he insisted in a deep growl.

'I know, because I *can* walk away.'

She easily pulled free from his grasp, turned and made it four steps back towards the cabin before he closed the distance between them. Bracing his arm against the wall, Sebastian crowded her from behind, feeling every inch of the Neanderthal he'd professed not to be. She stood loosely encased in his arms with her back to him, and he watched the rise and fall of her shoulders as she drew in breaths as deep as his own.

The heat rising from their bodies filled the space between them so much it was as if they were touching and he fought it. He fought himself. She turned her head halfway towards him, her eyes cast down as if just as reluctant as he, and he knew in his heart that if they shared a look it would all be over.

In the moonbeams he picked out the delicate eyelashes fanning her cheek, the hollow beneath her cheekbone and the slender curve to her neck, the slope of her shoulder and sweep of its blade. He studied every single inch of her in deep fascination, desperate to prolong the moment, to put off the final second of the internal war he was waging.

'You have to know that this has nothing to do with the painting,' he said, his defences weakening.

'I do,' she insisted quickly.

'I haven't finished,' he warned gently. 'Nothing to do with the painting, but time. This—whatever it is—can only be for the rest of our agreement. Do you understand?'

There was a pause before she responded and he was thankful for it. Because it meant she was thinking it through, truly appreciating that he meant there could be nothing beyond these twelve days.

'I do,' she whispered on an exhale.

'Then tell me you want this.' His voice was a harsh whisper as if he'd released the battle cry that had been sounding in his head.

'I want this.'

He placed his hand over hers, his fingers tangling with the silk and skin at her thigh. Her eyes drifted closed, her head slowly falling back in surrender.

'Promise me you'll tell me to stop if you want to stop,' he commanded in a whisper to her ear.

'I promise.'

And in that moment he knew he'd lost.

He'd lost the moment she'd had set her eyes on him, before he'd even looked across the bar in Victoriana.

He reached for her, turning her in his hands, her hips in his palms, sweeping her into his chest, and plundered a kiss from lips so soft and so open he thought he'd drown in them. The way she opened beneath him humbled him and he revered her with his hands and lips. The silk of her negligée skated over her skin beneath his palm as his thumb caught on her hip, pulling her into his body. His tongue delved into the welcome wet heat of her mouth and he wanted more. With a restraint and a patience almost unknown to him, he guided her through the doorway and walked her backwards to the bed without breaking the kiss.

Her hands roamed across his chest, leaving trails of branded skin, her short nails kneading into his arms and back, making him want to roar. Instead he pressed his lips against the curve of her neck, allowing his teeth to gently scrape against the sensitive skin there, relishing the shudder that shivered down her body and into his hands. She threw her head back in pleasure and he couldn't resist pressing open-mouthed kisses from her neck to her shoulder, gently moving the strap of her negligée aside, exposing just that bit more of her to him and drawing his attention to the way her taut nipples pulled at the silk across her chest.

Unable to stop himself, he took her covered breast in his hand, running his thumb over the stiff peak as he pressed kisses against the seam where skin met silk. She writhed like fire beneath his fingers and tongue and he wanted to consume every twist and turn of her, his pulse now like a drumbeat in his ear and mind.

She's mine, she's mine, she's mine.

Her own hand came up to the strap on her other shoulder, pulling at it, releasing the last thing holding up the silk between his skin and hers other than where it was caught in his hands at her chest. All he had to do was release her, release it, but he couldn't quite bring himself to do it yet. Her breasts, even covered, fitted perfectly within his hands, his mouth.

She shifted restlessly against him and he widened his stance as her legs instinctively slipped either side of his thigh. This time he couldn't help the growl that formed in his throat as she pressed against him and her moan sank into his skin. His hands flew to her shoulders, securing the straps beneath his palms, holding her back or drawing her closer, he didn't know any more.

His arousal pressed almost painfully against his trousers and he wanted nothing more than to tear the clothes from their bodies. But Sia was an innocent in the truest sense of the word and that meant that he put aside his own wants.

She looked glorious in his arms, her head cast back, the long trails of thick golden waves falling down her back almost reaching the base of her spine, her eyes having drifted shut as if lost in the sensual pleasure she was experiencing. He wished he could stop this moment in time, record the way she looked in this very moment. Because he had never seen anything more beautiful.

He couldn't help the curve to his lips as her eyes opened and she lifted her gaze to his. He gazed at her, trying to imprint this image on his mind, his memory, the gentle light cast by the moon shining on silk and catching in her hair. For a moment Sia seemed to study him in the same way and he wondered what she was thinking, what she was seeing. And then her hand came up around his neck and pulled his lips to hers and his mind went blank as he was lost to everything but the feeling of her tongue against his, her fingertips winding into his hair, the pull of his waistband from where her hand had sneaked between them.

Dios, he wanted her more than anything he'd ever wanted before. It was so much and so intense he struggled to keep the tremors from his touch. Finally, unable to take it any more, he released his hold on her arms and the straps caught beneath his palms and he watched, captivated, as the blue silk slid from her body and pooled at her feet, leaving her naked to the moonbeams and his scrutiny.

'I have no words,' he said, his gaze raking across every inch of beautiful smooth pale skin.

'You don't need words,' Sia said, reaching for the waistband of his trousers with a confidence that astounded him. Not because he didn't think her capable of it, but it was a confidence, a trust, that she had placed in him.

He caught her hand and held it against his chest for just a moment before he reached for her, picking her up and smiling as she instinctively wrapped her legs around his waist. He kneeled onto the bed, Sia still high in his arms, pressed against his chest, but able to look down on him, her hair coming about them like a curtain, cutting them off from the rest of the world.

He teased them both as he lowered her slightly, knowing she could feel the press of his erection through his trousers against her core. The way her eyes widened with expectation and want... He held her there until once again her eyes drifted closed and her body took over, her legs tightening their hold around his waist and leaning further into him to increase her own pleasure. The gasped inhale sharpened his arousal and he wanted to bury himself in her until he couldn't tell where he ended and she began. But Sia deserved, needed more than that.

Gently he laid her down, ruefully accepting the groan of disappointment that fell from her lips. He leaned back enough to remove his trousers and boxers, feeling her eyes on him the entire time. He stood there for a moment, allowing her to take him in, taking her in, in turn and marvelling how she reminded him of a Dante Gabriel Rossetti—her flowing auburn hair, pale skin...

His lips lifted gently as he saw the moment she began to grow self-conscious beneath his gaze and looked forward to the day she wouldn't. Until he realised that in all likelihood he would never see it.

He ignored the way his gut clenched at the thought and turned his attention to her feet. Picking one up, he kissed the arch of her foot and nipped at the soft flesh there when he heard Sia giggle. He lifted her leg gently, smoothing his hands along her calf, guiding her legs to either side of his to make room for him. The laughter left her lips and her eyes grew heavy with arousal as his hands swept further up. He relished the hitch in her breathing, mirroring his own, as he gently drew her legs further apart and settled his attention on the dusting of auburn curls at the apex of her thighs.

'Sia, I will stop *any* time,' he promised.

'Thank you.'

It was an exchange, an offer that had been accepted and it felt as if it was weighted with a trust that stretched beyond this moment and Sebastian refused to squander it. He placed open-mouthed kisses across her hip and downward until he found the soft, wet, enticing heat of her.

His tongue swirled around her clitoris and her hips bucked beneath him in euphoria. He placed his forearm across her hips, gently holding her in place, and sucked against her just as he entered her with his finger. Sia's breathing became tinged with small moans of delight, which only served to spur him on.

Her body shifted to welcome more of him, more of the pleasure he was bringing her and he relished it. Her body, her pleasure…it was more to him than his own. He could tell that she was on the brink of orgasm—the flush of her cheeks, the unseeing gaze—there was just a slim tether holding her back and he resented it as much as he imagined she did. He deepened his kiss between her thighs, brought two fingers to her entrance and thrust into her as he sucked on her clitoris and nearly came himself when he felt her orgasm against his mouth.

* * *

Sia came back down to earth gradually, but beneath the flickering moments were the traces of a feeling that had overwhelmed her entire body. She felt outside of herself, a giddy joy that almost made her laugh to think that such a feeling existed. She watched Sebastian through heavy-lidded eyes as he leaned back from the bedside table with something in his hand.

He put it aside and came down to lie beside her, running his palm from her hip up to her ribcage, over her breast and nipple and towards her neck to smooth away her hair from her shoulder, before placing kisses on the exact spot that made Sia want to hum with pleasure.

She leaned into the kiss as his arm came around her, pulling her back against the length of his body and the hardness of his arousal. Shocked by how much it turned her on, she couldn't help but shift against him, loving the way it felt to have his body encompassing hers.

'We can stop.'

'I don't want to.'

He gently pulled her round onto her back and when she looked him in the eye she could see that he was studying her, trying to seek out any hint of doubt.

'Sebastian, honestly. Am I nervous? A little. Excited? A lot. Scared? Not at all.' She reached up to cup his face, her palm against the slight stubble of his jaw. 'I want this,' she said before leaning up to place a kiss against his lips. And then another and another until mouths opened and tongues tangled and hands gripped and she was lost again.

Until she felt the loss of heat from his body and heard the tearing of foil even as he kissed her, his tongue filling her the way she wanted his body to. She shifted to welcome him between her legs and when his arms came up to frame her face she felt protected, cared for and she blinked against the sheen of tears threatening to form.

He kissed her then, long, slow and deliberate, easing away the last thread of nerves and distracting her with the sensual delight he was weaving between them. Seconds passed— minutes and time lost all meaning for Sia, who simply relished the power and passion of an endless kiss. Her body came alive, yearning and wanting, eager and impatient, her breathing quickened and her body flushed, heat tingling across her skin.

He positioned himself and gently pressed into her, gliding slowly deeper and deeper. She felt the unfamiliar tension of muscles building, the pressure strange and new, but his kiss was so different. He plundered her with his demanding tongue, filling her again and again with passion and power and it made her want more, need more. The aching desire building within her caused her to shift beneath him, to widen her legs, urging him deeper, harder into her so that his body would finally mirror his tongue, so that she would know what it felt like to be consumed by him completely.

Finally giving in to her desires, he pushed to the very depth and she felt him, all of him, and more, as if she no longer knew where he ended and she began. He withdrew and she nearly cried from the loss until he thrust back into her and she cried instead with pleasure. Again and again he thrust into her, her moans of ecstasy poured into him as he kissed her, their sweat-slicked bodies sliding effortlessly together, bringing them closer and closer to something unfathomable to Sia—a strange wordless moment that defied explanation. Each thrust took her nearer to the edge and further from rationality and she both longed for it and wanted to delay it because it would take her away from the sheer pleasure drenching her entire being.

Her hand slipped around Sebastian's waist instinctively, knowing what she wanted, pressing down against the base of his spine to hold him there, deep within her, as she shifted her hips, welcoming him further into her. His eyes grew wide, ringed with gold flecks that shone in the darkness, and in that second—the moment just before they both fell—they shared infinity.

CHAPTER EIGHT

SIA STIRRED, FEELING the warmth of a sunbeam against her skin, smiling to herself from the memory of the night before. She stretched out her legs, feeling the pull of unfamiliar muscles and the gentle hum of pleasure still in her body.

Reluctantly prising her eyes open, she spied the beautiful sunny day through the large open windows of the cabin. She also caught sight of a round table, pristine white cloth swaying in the breeze. From the bed she could make out platters of fruit, croissants and, thankfully, a large silver cafetière.

She realised that Sebastian wasn't there and was actually a little thankful to have just a moment to collect herself. She didn't for one minute regret what she'd done with him last night, but she was beginning to understand what he'd meant about unforeseen consequences.

The emotions that wrapped around how she felt about him and even herself were shifting in the sunlight like dust particles. There had been a moment last night when she had felt utterly connected to him. No masks, no lies, no secrets yet to be revealed. It had been just them and for a moment she'd thought—she'd imagined—they could have...

The rest of their lives.

And then she kicked off the sheets as if she could kick away the thought as pure fancy, even if somewhere deep in her heart she clung to the possibility. She had agreed only to the next twelve days—eleven now, she realised as she ducked into the shower and stretched beneath the soothing hot jets of water cascading over her skin. It shouldn't have been arousing, but the memory of Sebastian's hands and lips doing the very same thing heated her blood and she twisted the handle to cold, relishing the sharp shock and clearing the sensual fog from her mind.

Laughing at herself a little, she reached for a towel, dried herself and then took the silk robe hanging beside the shower. As she walked out towards the decking, fastening the robe at her waist, she took in the signs of what had happened last night. At the foot of the bed she picked up her silk negligée from the floor, running it through her hands as she looked out to the decking and the feast on the table. Condensation had formed on the glass jug of freshly squeezed orange juice and the pang in her stomach prodded her into action.

She sat in the place opposite a cup that still held an inch of rapidly cooling coffee, her frown dissolving as she bit into the most delicious flaky pastry, uncaring that she groaned out loud, especially with no one to hear her. Not even halfway through it, she was already eyeing another, contemplating just how wicked it would be to have a second. Sebastian had made her wanton and as her tongue flicked out to rescue a sliver of sweet almond she couldn't bring herself to care.

Although there was a slight sense of unease building as she considered the range of emotions Sebastian might be feeling. Did he regret it? Had it been *okay* for him? The wisp of concern at that thought was immediately soothed by the memory of the look in his eyes last night, the awe that she'd felt reflected back at her in his gaze…that wasn't fake.

She held the rim of her coffee cup against

her lip, unseeing of the horizon or the beautiful blue sea peppered with boats at varying distances from shore until a small speedboat caught her eye. Not because of the speed at which it was going but the figure at the helm. Tall, proud and focused, there was something about the man that made her think of Sebastian as the boat cut through the waves.

Without thinking, she went into the room to retrieve the binoculars from the table and, returning to the decking, brought them to her face, startled by the detail she could see.

The wind rippled across his white shirt, flicked through his hair and pressed against his tan trousers, outlining powerful thighs. For a moment she was distracted by the sight, her senses still alert from the night before. Until her gaze snagged on two large dark shapes on the floor by his feet and she remembered the duffel bags they'd waited for at the airfield back in London.

Sebastian passed a catamaran and several jet skiers, ignoring their greetings, his focus zeroed in on a beautiful yacht way out in the distance, far enough for the two figures waiting on the boat to seem tiny even with the binoculars.

Unable to look away, it was some minutes before Sebastian met the yacht, pulling up alongside to pass something to them which could have been the duffel bags. After a brief exchange Sebastian manoeuvred the speedboat around and turned back to shore.

Sia put the binoculars to the side and picked up her coffee cup, her mind purposely blank. Automatically she finished the croissant, no longer under its sugary sway. She must have sat like that for quite some time because she stirred only when she heard footsteps on the pathway and saw Sebastian approaching the steps to the cabin.

His lips quirked into a broad smile and he removed the sunglasses to reveal eyes sparkling with sensual mischief. He closed the distance between them and before she could finish her breath had placed a firm kiss against her lips.

'I was hoping to find you in bed,' he said.

'I could say the same,' she replied, purposely keeping her tone neutral.

'Oh, that,' he replied as she saw his eyes skate across the table and over the binoculars. 'A couple of guys sailing the islands underestimated how much fuel they'd need. I didn't want to bother the staff in their preparations for the opening, so I headed out and gave them enough to get where they were going.'

'Very kind of you.'

'You sound surprised,' he remarked with a raised eyebrow.

'Not in the slightest,' she said, unable to resist the smile pulling at her lips.

He leaned in and stole another kiss. 'I don't believe you.' Grabbing an apple from the bowl, he took a bite. 'Finish breakfast because we have to get going.'

'Going where?' she asked, intrigued in spite of herself.

'You'll see,' he teased and disappeared inside the cabin, from where she heard the shower start. But out on the veranda the smile loosened its hold and a cloud passed over the sun, chilling the air, and Sia shivered.

Sebastian loved the speedboat. The feel of the engine roaring behind him, the feel of the wheel beneath his palm, the stinging heat from the sun soothed by the cool air buffeting them as they cut through the waves. And he wasn't the only one. The look of excitement in Sia's eyes, the exhilarated yell each time they crossed and crested a wave unexpectedly, the juddering bump both startling and delighting.

Everything he'd set out to achieve in the Caribbean was done. The party celebrating and thanking the hotel staff and contributors had been a roaring success. The feedback from the visiting staff had been not only good but useful and he had a team working out whether it should be an annual event for all staff and hotels.

And now he could put the business with the painting behind him. He was surprised to find a sense of relief. Perhaps that was what had been missing when he'd toasted Aliah in Victoriana. The line in the sand. Everyone now had their due and their own piece of revenge.

Not everyone, his inner voice chided.

Sia might not have a job or a career to return to when their time together concluded. Not that she should return to a company as rotten as Bonnaire's, but still.

'Fancy taking her for a spin?' he asked Sia,

while wondering if perhaps there was something he could do about that.

'Really?'

'Sure. It's not as if there's a lot of traffic out here for you to hit,' he said, gesturing to the acres of crystal-blue sea around them. She practically jumped off the seat in her eagerness and Sebastian couldn't help but smile. When he'd returned to find her at breakfast, for a moment he'd wondered... There had been a look in her eyes, but it had disappeared since then.

Shutting that thought down, he brought her in between his body and the wheel, encasing her within his arms, and smiled when she looked up at him.

'What do I do?'

'Aim for that small island over there,' he said, placing her hands on the wheel. 'Have a bit of a go—*gently*,' he said as she squeaked and the boat veered off to the left. He guided the wheel back on course. 'You got it?' She nodded, her expression fierce with concentration, allowing him to stand back a little and enjoy.

It's just for now, he told himself. Just for the next two weeks. Because after that, whether she returned to Bonnaire's or not, whether she mi-

raculously found either the proof or the painting, she'd be gone from his life. And he was
happy with that, he told himself fiercely. He
was good at indulging momentary pleasures
and that was what Sia was. An incredible, impressive woman but she was only in his life
for the next eleven days. He'd done serious,
he'd buckled down when he'd needed to, he'd
played the parent, even. And no matter what
kind of promise he saw in Sia's eyes, he would
not willingly return to that.

The wind whipped at the white linen top Sia
wore over her orange bikini. He couldn't help
but smile. That morning, when he'd presented
her with it, rather than questioning it or hesi-
tating, she ran her eyes over it in wonder, the
smile pulling at her lips one of excited expectation. A look he wanted to see much more of
from her.

'Sebastian?' Sia called over the roaring wind,
pulling him from his thoughts.

They were approaching the island and he took
the wheel, keeping her encircled in his arms.
'Perfect. Thank you, Chief Mate,' he said.

'If you expect me to say *aye-aye*, or call you Captain then—'

Sia broke off at the sudden, shocking heat in Sebastian's gaze that threatened to consume them both in its ferocity even as he powered down the boat.

'Really?' she teased. 'You want me to—'

And then all she could do was scream as he scooped her up in his arms and jumped them both overboard, the warm water soothing on wind and sun-kissed skin, his arms around her as he trod water to keep them above the surface.

'You look like a mermaid,' he said as she pushed the wet ropes of her hair back from her face, before putting her arms around his neck, leaning in and pressing her lips against his, the warm salty water making her bold. He held her against him, allowing her to explore him, her fingers travelling around his strong neck and shoulders, her legs around his waist, his thighs supporting her. She wanted nothing more, to think of nothing more, no doubts, no needs, just want. Just him.

He carried her all the way to the shore, where they had a picnic on the beach of cold potted shrimp with mango salad, bacon-wrapped crab bites, salmon rillettes, smoky seared octopus, fresh green lemony salad and beautiful breads with butter and a bottle of chilled white wine. They snorkelled, swam, laughed and kissed and not once did Sia think of Sebastian's morning boat trip, the lost painting or her job.

Because this loose and easy way of living... She was beginning to really fall for it.

INTERVIEWER ONE: *So let me get this right. You went to the Caribbean, where you attended a VIP party with no VIPs, went snorkelling, swimming and had a picnic? Did you even look for the painting? I mean, separate rooms at least would have allowed you some time alone—did you not investigate at all?*

MS KEATING: *I no longer believed that he had the painting with him in the Caribbean.*

INTERVIEWER TWO: *But did you ask him?*

MS KEATING: *If he had the painting?*

INTERVIEWER TWO: *No, about his mother.*

Sia followed Sebastian back to the cabin, her fingers tangled with his, her body happily exhausted from swimming and snorkelling and her heart satiated with happiness. She caught sight of a barbecue set up on the decking.

'I hope you don't mind. The restaurant is now closed so that they can prepare for opening next week. You're going to have to put up with my cooking.'

'You cook?' she asked, genuinely surprised.

'Not at all,' he said without shame, 'but putting a piece of meat on a grill and presenting dishes that other people have prepared is hardly cooking.'

She laughed at his honest response. She went to the shower to wash off the sea salt, strangely relishing the moments she had to herself. Having Sebastian intent on her in this way was overwhelming—and, she warned herself, temporary. Her empty fist clenched, remembering how good it had felt to have her fingers entwined with his. She couldn't let this be more than what it was. She couldn't let herself feel more than what she should.

Determined to keep a little of herself back from him this time, Sia put on a bright smile as she made her way out to the decking. The dress she'd chosen was forest-green with a thin shoulder strapped lace bodice that stopped just beneath her breasts and fell down to her ankles with silky skirts. She felt both Grecian and bohemian, her hair drying in thick waves from the shower and her feet bare.

As she reached the decking, Sebastian had his back to her, focusing on the steak he was cooking. The marinade smelt incredible, making her mouth water just as much as he had in the shower.

'Would you pour the wine?' Sebastian said without turning.

She reached for the red, noticing the label.

'You know it?' he asked.

'Heard of it, never tasted,' she replied of the Tersi branded Pinot Noir.

'You couldn't be tempted?'

'I couldn't afford it,' she replied on a sigh as she poured out the light, fruity wine into two glasses. He really did live in a very different world to her, one that she doubted very much she belonged in.

She took a seat at the table, laid—as promised—with beautiful dishes, salads and vegetables, and smiled when Sebastian returned to the table victorious with two perfectly cooked steaks. Gentle conversation, the warmth of the wine, delicious food and the promise of later behind nearly every look or touch from Sebastian lulled Sia into a state of relaxed bliss.

As he gathered the plates and cleared the table, she looked out at the sun, lazily setting on the horizon, slashing ochre and burnt sienna across the division between sea and sky. It felt almost as if it could be just the two of them at the edge of the world. It was magical. And for the first time in what felt like years she had the urge to pick up a paintbrush. To capture the moment, the *entire* moment, the feeling as much as the view, the slight sense of tearing within in her between sadness and sheer joy.

'You okay?' Sebastian asked and she realised that he'd been sitting there for some time.

'Yes. A nearly perfect day,' she proclaimed.

'Nearly?' Sebastian countered, full of mock outrage.

She couldn't help but think back to the start of the day. To his trip to the yacht and his explanation. *I'm very good at spotting fakes.*

'What would your perfect day look like?' he asked, bringing her out of her thoughts.

'A private viewing of the *Allegory of Fame* by Artemisia Gentileschi,' she replied without hesitation.

'Really? Why that artist and painting?'

'The artist is my namesake.'

'Your full name is *Artemisia*?' he asked, the shock in his voice almost amusing.

'Yup. Try that on for size at primary school,' she said, the sting of childhood taunts still sharp years on. Even more so after her father's arrest.

'You don't like it?'

'Hardly. I consider it his worst act of parental cruelty.'

'Above getting arrested?'

'Absolutely. It was about *him*. *His* favourite artist. *His* arrogance and obsession with the greats.'

Sebastian looked out at the sea, a slight frown on his brow.

'You said your father named you after his favourite artist because of his arrogance?' he asked, and she nodded. 'Could it have been that he saw something in you, even as a baby, that reminded him of Artemisia?'

It was not something that Sia had considered before.

'You know her story?' Sebastian asked. 'What she overcame to become one of the most accomplished Baroque painters of the seventeenth century?'

'Of course,' she said, calling to mind the difficulties the artist had experienced, but also how afterwards she had thrived and flourished.

'Then is it beyond the realm of imagination that your father would name you after such an incredible woman because he sensed those same traits in you?'

Sebastian allowed her to sit with her thoughts while he rose to retrieve the wine and topped up their glasses.

'So, what is it about *Allegory of Fame* that is so significant for you?'

Pushing her musings aside, Sia couldn't help but smile as the image of a painting she knew like the back of her hand rose in her mind. 'It's a remarkable painting, but in a private collection even the Bonnaire's name won't allow me to access. Fame—depicted as a woman—isn't portrayed as being classically beautiful. She's not Titian, or half naked, she's not under some intense sensual sway or an object for male appreciation. She is handsome, powerful in her own right, and there's a look on her face... She seems to be watching something happening off the canvas and her acceptance of it is striking. As if it's shocking, sad, but also unsurprising.' She realised that Sebastian was looking at her in a strange way. 'Sorry, that sounds fanciful.'

'Not at all. It's your perfect day to do with as you please. Did you always want to be an art valuer?'

'I always wanted to be in the arts,' she said, skirting around his question. 'It was more than just following in my father's footsteps. I wasn't lying when I said it was in my blood; turpentine and oil paints flow through my veins,' she confided ruefully.

'Did you ever want to paint?'

'Yes,' she said, remembering her childhood obsession with colour, with recreating images in her mind, light and shade, depth and composition. The expression of meaning and emotion beyond language, which cried out and screamed in colour and texture. She could feel it rising within her now as if Sebastian had set off an avalanche within her and she was beginning to feel everything, feel too much.

'Why didn't you?'

'I...' Sia considered all the possible answers and felt a wave of tiredness at constantly filtering her words as if they might be used against her in whatever game it was they were playing. She wasn't sure she wanted to play it any more. So she told the truth. 'I was afraid. Of only being able to copy artists like my father. Of not having any natural talent myself.' She realised then that it was a little like her fear of passion...that she might have inherited both her parents' worst traits. But hadn't Sebastian shown her a way around that? To navigate that fear, access her own passion and *not* be like her mother?

What might art school have looked like if she'd not let her fears in there too? Unable or unwilling to face the answer to that question, she turned to him.

'What about you?'

'What *about* me? I have eleven hotels, a combined total of seventy-two stars, many of which are Michelin—'

'I know,' she interrupted, slightly frustrated

at his almost standard response. 'But…is this what you really want? Please don't get me wrong,' she stated quickly, sensing that Sebastian was growing annoyed. 'I don't mean to question you on it, but you're just going to keep opening more and more hotels? Make more and more money? I'm not disparaging what you've achieved, Sebastian, because it's incredible and it has clearly supported your family to a great extent. But—' she searched for something that would pin down what she meant, what she was looking for, his hopes and dreams, not obligations and responsibilities '—what did you want to be as a child?' she finally asked. 'Astronaut? Deep-sea diver? Surely you wanted to be more than…'

And then she could have bitten off her own tongue. She genuinely hadn't meant to belittle his accomplishments, as if somehow being a billionaire was distasteful, but she couldn't shake the feeling that it wasn't, perhaps never had been, what he'd intended to be. She took a mouthful of wine, hoping to swallow some of the guilt and shame.

'I was going to be a doctor. I'd got into Harvard Medical School.'

Her heart broke at the way he said it. As if he'd meant to pick something up on a shopping list and forgot it. No big deal. But it was precisely that which told her how much of a sacrifice it had been.

'After the exile I couldn't afford to go, and I wouldn't leave Maria. Eduardo was barely capable of holding his head up and Valeria was too busy bemoaning her fate of being married to an ex-Duke, so neither would have been able to look after her. Do you like the wine?'

The swift about-turn of the conversation nearly gave her whiplash.

'I do. It's delicious.'

'Theo will be glad to hear that,' he said before she could try and steer the conversation back. Instead, she let him have the space he needed.

'You know the vintner?'

'A very good friend of mine.'

'You have friends?' she teased, trying for levity.

'You seem surprised,' he observed wryly, taking a sip of the wine.

'No,' she replied easily. 'I'm just curious as to what they'd think of you stealing a painting worth one hundred million pounds.'

'Is that your question for today?' he replied around a smile.

'No,' she said, her tone suddenly serious, thinking back to what he had said last night. Was it really only last night? It felt as if so much had passed since then.

The look in Sebastian's eyes told her that he was thinking of the same thing. She heard his sigh taken away by the gentle breeze of the night and waited. Because she couldn't help but think that his response, *this* response, would be the answer to nearly all of her questions.

Sebastian knew what she wanted, knew that they would work their way around to this question at some point. It almost felt like a relief to finally address it.

'The first time I met Durrántez was in his studio. My mother had taken me. She'd just found out she was pregnant and, it's trite but true, she had this glow about her. Everything felt—' he shrugged '—bigger. Not physically, but her emotions. Her love. It was as if they had grown to encompass Maria before she was even there. And for those few months of her pregnancy I relished in it, rejoiced even.

'Durrántez was in his seventies when he

painted *Woman in Love*. He had this full head of thick white hair,' he said, gesturing in the air with his hand as if frothing the man's hair in his imagination. 'Thick black-rimmed glasses and a blue paint-covered shirt. Half of his studio was a mess and the other half was almost military in its precision.'

'My father was the same,' Sia said, smiling as if she could imagine what he was remembering. 'He said it was the order that made the creativity possible.'

Sebastian nodded, thinking that it seemed to fit with Etienne's slightly erratic but always passionate persona.

'Even Durrántez seemed to have fallen under her spell. They would talk for hours about artists, arguing over who was the greater in each decade, first by painter and then by painting.' The memory of their voices, heated with passion and then deflated by laughter, rose up over the gentle cooing of Caribbean birds and he was back in Spain. 'I could see it, you know? In the way that he looked at her. It was the way anyone who loved her looked at her. As if my mother were not only the centre of the room but of the universe. She had a laugh that would attract attention and a way about her that would make her as amiable to prince or pauper.'

'It sounds quite a bit like you,' Sia observed, her eyes shining in the darkness.

Sebastian shrugged it off, half wanting to share something, anything, with his mother and half wanting to remember that ability as uniquely hers.

'I was ten at the time and it was during the summer holidays. I had brought a book, expecting it to be boring and dull, but I couldn't help but watch every minute of it. And now I'm glad of it. My mother sat for Durrántez for a total of seventeen hours and for every minute of it, like Durrántez, I traced the line of my mother's smile, the curve of her cheek, the warm blush of happiness and I assessed the colour of her eyes. I'll never forget my mother's face, even if my sister wasn't the spitting image of her.'

Goosebumps rose over Sia's skin as she realised what Sebastian was saying and she felt tears press at the corners of her eyes.

'The painting was completed after her death. In the sittings she'd been wearing a white dress. But in the finished painting Durrántez changed it to black. A mark of respect, a mark of loss—his, ours, I'll never know, but it was a mark nonetheless. It was the last painting that Durrántez ever painted.'

For nearly twenty years no one had identified the model for *Woman in Love* and, for some reason, Sia found herself wanting desperately to keep that secret. A sense of loss, greater than she'd ever personally experienced, rose up within her chest as she realised that his mother must have died giving birth to his sister, perhaps only weeks or less after she had sat for the painting. Loss of a mother, of a muse for a painter, of a powerful presence who'd debated great artists, the loss of a future that Sebastian had clearly wanted, because of his father's own stupidity.

'How did the Sheikh end up with the...?' She didn't need to finish the question. She began to see how the threads came together as if she had just unravelled a knot she'd been struggling with for days. 'The Sheikh was the business partner who convinced your father to invest his money and the money of others. Oh,' she said, the shock finally settling—the moment she realised that his father had used the portrait of his mother as financial collateral. The sense of betrayal Sebastian must have felt causing her to shake her head as if trying to deny such a thing.

'And Abrani never let you buy it? Even though he must have known how important that was to you?' Sia was no longer seeing the beauty of the sunset, the way the rich forest-green palms swayed in the breeze. She was forging pathways in her mind, making connections... 'So you got the painting back. But it wouldn't have been enough to steal the painting, would it? Because, although you *wanted* the painting, it wasn't really about that. It was about publicly shaming the Sheikh. Or perhaps giving him the choice?

'He could always have insisted that the painting was authentic, but he'd end up facing an investigation that could reveal his own duplicity in the oil deal ten years ago. Or he could accept the public shame for trying to sell a fake.

'But, in order to achieve any of this, the painting *had to be seen* as a fake. Otherwise, it would never have come back on the Sheikh.'

And it would have the double impact of punishing Bonnaire's for getting involved in backdoor auctions and dodgy dealings, Sia realised, her head spinning. Now that she could see the pieces, how they fitted together, emotions began to pour through the cracks. Her heart ached for the young boy who had first lost his mother and then later lost his home, his future. She could see the sacrifices Sebastian had made for his family and understood his penchant for indulgence now. She could taste a desire for revenge on her own tongue.

But what that meant for her, for what she was trying to do here... Her head began to spin.

'It is an interesting hypothesis,' he said, watching her very closely. And she knew why. She could feel it just as much as him. The turning point. The moment that would define their future. 'It is a shame that you've used up your questions for today and therefore I can't confirm or deny.'

His gaze locked on hers, as if both questioning and insisting. Sia nodded slowly.

She could walk away now. She might not have proof, she might not have even seen the painting, but she'd been wrong when she'd told him in Victoriana that she didn't care why he'd stolen the painting. Because suddenly the why had become the most important thing about this whole mess. Neither Bonnaire's nor Abrani *deserved* to have the real painting returned, so the only person to lose out would be her.

Or she could take Sebastian up on his offer. Remain in the game for at least another twenty-four hours, this strange bubble of hypotheticals that felt incredibly far removed from real life— real life with a horrible job she might no longer have, living in a miserable flat she'd never liked, hiding from a passion she had refused to acknowledge and a desire to do something… *more* than valuing paintings for other people.

She turned to Sebastian, away from the questions, away from the world outside. She wanted to feel his touch, feel the truth of it, because it was so much easier than working out the lies that had been told to her and that she had told to herself.

'Take me to bed?' she asked.

'Your wish is my command,' he said, taking her hand and kissing her palm. 'For as long as you will it.'

CHAPTER NINE

INTERVIEWER ONE: *Okay...so snorkelling—
tick—sunbathing—tick—swimming—tick.
Gorgeous food, stunning sunsets and walks
on the beach—we get it. But we know you
didn't stay in the Caribbean for the whole
time.*

MS KEATING: *Really?*

INTERVIEWER TWO: *We are investigators.*

MS KEATING: *[silence]*

INTERVIEWER ONE: *When did you get to
Italy?*

SIA HAD BEEN reluctant to leave the Caribbean
but the prospect of going to Italy had her practically skipping down the steps of the private
jet that had whisked them to an airfield just
outside Siena.

'I can't believe you haven't been to Italy,' Sebastian said as if disgusted. 'It is a crime.'

'Your definition of crime might need to be looked at,' she replied around a smile.

'Anywhere you would like to go?' he asked, guiding her towards a beautiful grey convertible at the end of the tarmac. It was sleek and old-fashioned, the kind of car that made Sia want to run her hand across the bonnet to see if it was as silky as it looked, gleaming in the Tuscan sun.

'Is this yours?' she demanded, momentarily forgetting his question.

'Yes.'

'Can I drive?' she asked.

'Absolutely not.'

'But you flew the plane,' she said, knowing full well that she sounded like a stroppy child.

'Really? That's how you're going to play this?' Sebastian demanded, peering over the top of his sunglasses.

'Fine.' She relented long enough to return to his earlier question. 'I want to go to the Uffizi and the Galleria dell'Accademia in Florence. Definitely have to see the medieval frescoes in the Basilica di San Francesco in Assisi, and

Michelangelo's *Pieta* in St Peter's Basilica in Vatican City—'

'Okay, okay, I get it,' Sebastian interrupted, putting the car into gear and pulling out of the airfield onto the road towards his estate just outside of Siena. 'You want to see everything.'

'If we can,' she said, a hint of reticence in her voice for the first time in days.

'We've got time,' Sebastian said, as if trying to convince himself as he shifted up to the highest gear and hit the accelerator.

The glide of the steering wheel beneath his hands as they took the familiar corners and bends in the road to his estate was strangely satisfying to Sebastian. It hadn't been that long since he'd been here, but for the first time it felt as if he were coming home. For so many years, on the move between his hotels all around the world, working every hour he could, it had been a place more for Maria than him. But, bringing Sia here, it felt as if he were revealing part of himself to her.

But only a part.

He could afford her this small glimpse into his life because she was going to leave it. They only had ten days left now and it was because he felt that time was running out for them that he'd decided to surprise her that evening.

He smiled, the prospect of it exciting him as much as he hoped it would delight her. He looked across to where she sat beside him. Having tied a scarf around her hair to stop it whipping about her head, she looked like a siren from the silver screen, the bright slash of red lipstick screaming from rosebud lips that he wanted very much to mess up with deep, hot, open-mouthed kisses.

She looked glorious. Alive and full of even more passion than he'd thought possible when he'd first met her in Victoriana. He wanted it, all of it. His fingers gripped the steering wheel and he wondered when this obsession with her would be done. His need for her was almost constant, but it was absolutely nothing in comparison with his awareness of what *she* needed and wanted.

'When was the last time you were home?' Sia asked in a half shout over the roar of the wind and the purr of the engine.

'I had a little lunch thing with the Queen of Iondorra and her husband,' he said.

'Did you just name-drop a royal?' she demanded.

'Absolutely,' he said, shrugging his shoulder, causing Sia to laugh. 'It's one of the perks of Theo's marriage.'

'Theo?'

'Tersi. The friend you were surprised I had?' He paused to take the last turn-off for the estate. 'We were checking out Maria's husband. Needed to make sure that he was good enough,' he said as he drove parallel to the boundary wall of his home.

'And was he?'

'Time will tell,' Sebastian replied, turning his mind away from Matthieu Montcour as he guided the car through the wrought iron gates and up the drive before pulling to a stop beside the steps leading up to the front door.

Sia took her time getting out of the beautiful sports car she'd enjoyed so much, partly because her legs felt a little unsteady and partly because Sebastian might as well have brought her to the house of her dreams. Only it was more of a grand estate than a house.

Two storeys high and what looked like at least

six rooms wide, the beautiful stone building stood, box like, against a background of beautifully manicured greenery dotted with lazy bees and butterflies. She almost laughed. She needed someone to pinch her but wanted to stay in this strange place that she could so easily fall in love with. She feared falling back down to earth with a very harsh bump.

Sebastian had paused halfway up the steps and, perfectly framed by the three arched domes in the centre of the estate's façade, looked at her as if *she* were on display rather than his wealth, his home…his sanctuary.

She walked around the car, over to where his hand was outstretched, and braced herself for the tingles and shivers that his touch always caused. He led her through the front door and down a terracotta-floored corridor. Shafts of sunlight fell on the tiles from the door at the end, making the hallway feel warm and rich and welcoming. She passed an office on the right-hand side, just before a staircase that clung to the side of the hallway leading to the upper level. On the left, she could see a large living area with a fireplace and mantel that drew her gaze, but Sebastian kept on towards the door at the back and the moment that she followed him through the door she could see why.

It was spectacular. She felt as if she'd sneaked into paradise.

A table and two chairs in white wrought iron were set with lunch and a pitcher of what looked like cool lemonade, the scent of sweet citrus hanging in the air. The borders were lush with large evergreens in silver and blue, box trees had been proudly manicured into appealing shapes and large pots of bay created a path to where purple wisteria hung over a metal arch above the table to provide shade from the strong summer's sun.

'And this just happened to be here waiting for us?'

'Not at all. I would imagine my very good staff spent hours slaving over hot stoves to present you with this feast.'

They reached the table and she inhaled the beautiful scent of fresh garden herbs.

'Me?'

Sebastian grimaced. 'Are you happy to amuse yourself for an hour or so? I have business to attend to,' he said, cupping her chin with his hand, his thumb pressed gently against the centre of her bottom lip. In an instant the fire that was always there, waiting to be fanned into life, roared.

Reluctantly, he let her go. 'You can go anywhere you like in the estate, apart from the basement.' Then he kissed her on the forehead and, before Sia could even think to ask any questions, he disappeared.

It was the first time Sebastian had gone against their agreement. He'd promised her that nothing in his life would be off-limits, yet in seconds the excitement that she had felt at being in Italy, at being in Sebastian's home had turned to ash, making her stomach ache and killing her appetite.

It was that same seesawing feeling that she got when something was wrong. Like the way she'd felt when she'd seen Sebastian take the boat out to the yacht. She pressed her hand against her stomach, trying to soothe the feeling away with gentle circles.

Was it a double bluff, perhaps? Did he think that she was going to search the house for the painting? Did he *want* her to focus on the basement rather than another part of the house in the hope that she might miss something hiding in plain sight? No matter what happened between them, she couldn't lose sight of why she was here. Her job. Returning with the painting or with proof. Even if the lines of who was right and who was wrong had become blurred. Even if she thought Sebastian might have already stolen something far more precious to her than the painting.

Sia started on the second floor of the house and she couldn't help but remember doing the same thing in the house in Knightsbridge. Only this actually felt like a home. The colours were mostly earthy in tone, warm terracotta, soothing cream, soft greys from natural stone and wood. The fresh life-giving green from the outside had been brought inside by trailing indoor ivy in the bathrooms, which loved being near the large, bright, south-facing windows. The powerful midday sun beamed into spacious bedrooms, each taking their colour cues from one large dominant painting. It all called to an unknown yearning within Sia. A yearning for something so much like this.

The paintings reminded her of the ones by

Astou Ndiaye, most by seemingly unknown artists but each were exquisite, stunning and mostly abstract, as seemed to be Sebastian's preference, and her mind began to wander away from Durrántez and instead to Sebastian. Was it jealousy she was beginning to feel as she wondered what it would have been like to be 'discovered' by Sebastian? To have a patron who believed in her art, in her and what she could achieve? But, even as she had the thought, she bit her lip and realised that perhaps she *did* know what that felt like—to be discovered by him, to be encouraged and championed, to be challenged and to rise to meet that challenge.

Not the challenge of this game they seemed to be playing. It went deeper than that as, no matter what might happen with the painting, Sia couldn't deny that she had been changed by him, made to question herself, her job, her choices. And rightly so.

She was about to leave the upper floor when the sound of wheels on the gravel drive drew her attention to the window looking out on the front of the estate. There was a large grey van and several men in uniforms stepped out and walked to where Sebastian was ready to greet them.

She couldn't hear what they were saying, but she could see them shaking hands and nodding. The uniformed men went to the back of the van and Sebastian stood back as they removed something. It was a reasonably small wooden crate, the kind used to store and move paintings. The kind that was the perfect size for the Durrántez.

Her heart clenched and her skin prickled painfully. Was he planning to sneak it into the estate without her knowing? Did he intend to keep it hidden in the basement or would he share it with her? And if he did, what then?

As her mind raced through the possible implications she realised that seeing the painting would make it real. That she'd finally have to make a choice. In the last week she'd been living out the most beautiful fantasy—one of incredible experiences and impossible pleasures. But it was just that. A fantasy.

But if he shared the painting with her then the fantasy would disappear and she'd be forced to choose between him and the painting. And for the first time since this whole thing started she wasn't sure what to do.

She stood looking out of the window long after Sebastian had disappeared inside with the crate, after the men in uniforms had driven away and long after Sebastian's allotted 'hour or so' had passed as she contemplated whether the fantasy was one he'd invited her to step into or one he'd enticed her in to, to cover his tracks.

Sebastian felt a twinge of uncertainty. He'd not seen Sia that afternoon though, in all fairness, he'd been distracted by a minor wrangling in the New York hotel and by the time it had been resolved it was nearly five p.m. He'd thought she might have found herself something to do, or been resting, but as the day drew into dusk he couldn't quite shake the feeling that, despite his best intentions, the evening might not quite go as planned. He'd known that telling her an area of the estate was off-limits was a risk, but had decided it was worth it. Something he still believed.

When Sia finally arrived in the living room she took his breath away. The dress was of a similar style to the one she had worn in Vic-

toriana, but this one was the colour of honey.
Rich, alluring, evocative. As if she'd dressed
with the sole purpose of driving him out of his
mind. Which was why it took him a moment
to see that Sia was braced, as if ready for some
kind of hurt, and he couldn't quite tell why.

'Are you okay?' he said, fighting the urge to
close the distance between them, instinctively
knowing that it could cause her to flee.

'Yes.'

Sebastian bit his tongue. Clipped, one-word
answers weren't Sia's usual style. Giving in
to temptation, he crossed the room, stopping
barely a foot from her. Sia couldn't meet his
gaze and he closed down the bitter laugh he
felt rising. He hadn't been exaggerating when
he'd declared her a terrible actress. In an instant he knew what she had thought of his re-
quest, what conclusion she'd drawn. And could
he deny that she was right to do so? Justified,
even, after everything he'd done?

He took a breath. 'I had a plan. For how this
evening would go. But...' He trailed off, realising that it didn't matter what he said, how he
might explain things. The only way would be to
show her. 'Come with me?' he asked, his hand

held out just like he had done hours before. She nodded, only this time she didn't take his hand, leaving his fingers to close on thin air.

Pushing down on a feeling he refused to name, he led her to the door to the basement, flicking on the lights for the staircase and taking the lead. 'The previous owners converted the entire area into a *very* expensive wine cellar,' he said, all the while questioning why he was persevering with this. Anything he'd hoped to gain was now well and truly shot to pieces. 'But with a few tweaks I realised it would be perfect,' he said as he reached the bottom of the stairs.

'Perfect for what?'

'This,' he said, turning on the low lighting that instantly brought warmth and light to the cavernous underground chamber. The space stretched beyond the footprint of the estate, almost all the way to the boundary. It could have been a World War One weapons bunker for all he knew, but it had been exactly what he'd wanted for his collection.

He was strangely satisfied by the gasp of surprise that fell from Sia's lips. He'd fallen in love with it the moment he'd seen it and it had been the sole reason for buying the estate. Beautiful sand-coloured stone slabs made up the flooring that met aged brick, running along, up and over the walls and curved ceiling of the basement. Soft blond up-lighting mirrored the arches in the walls that led through to other rooms and areas that ran off the central corridor stretching before them. It was his pride and joy and he'd been so excited to share it with Sia, but the moment he'd seen that look in her eyes, the fear of what he might reveal to her, he knew he only had himself to blame.

The space was what Sia noticed first. The walls she noticed second. Paintings. Everywhere she could see. Paintings by unspeakably famous artists, some that she'd only ever heard of and some she could have sworn were hanging in museums and galleries visited by tourists every day. She left Sebastian to walk through the stone corridors and arched hallways, her mind lit with wonder at the most incredible private art collection she'd ever seen. There didn't seem to be a particular pattern, subject matter or epoch to curate the paintings, other than 'famous' and 'priceless'.

She noticed that the temperature wasn't cold, nor too hot, Sebastian clearly taking great care of a collection that's value increased with every single new painting she saw. It made her head swim.

Further into the space she came to a stop.

On the far wall was a small square of velvet covering a painting. There was even a little golden rope attached to it, as if for some grand reveal. Her pulse spiked and leapt, her heart thudding wildly. She was scared. Scared that it was the Durrántez, scared that it wasn't. Now the moment had arrived she still didn't know what to do.

There was a table in front of the painting and it felt strange, inappropriate almost. As was the bottle of champagne gathering condensation, waiting to fill the two empty glass flutes on the ivory tablecloth. The whole thing felt absurd, as if he were making even more of a joke of her and it hurt—the idea that whatever was behind the cover was some form of entertainment.

Sebastian hadn't said a word, remaining behind as if leaving her to face it by herself. Sia felt his eyes on her as she slowly walked towards the velvet cover, conscious of the way her dress shifted over her skin, the way the wedge of her shoe felt against the slight un-evenness of the stone flooring, causing her hips to sway, the awareness straightening her spine, and she gently stretched her shoulders back as if determined to meet her fate head-on.

She reached for the golden cord and even be-fore she'd pulled strongly enough on it to lower the velvet she knew.

It wasn't the Durrántez.

'*Allegory of Fame* by Artemisia Gentiles-chi,' she heard him explain unnecessarily as she took in the painting she'd always wanted to see.

It was breathtaking in the truest sense. Sia's eyes hungrily consumed every inch of the small painting—the richness of Fame's dress, the golden trumpet in her grip, the angle of her head as she leaned to one side... It sounded so mundane but in reality, in *person* it was in-credible.

And it was not the Durrántez. No. It was the thing she had told Sebastian she would want for her perfect day. Which made sense of the table behind her, the chilled champagne, the exclusive, intimate private viewing of a paint-

ing that she'd always wanted to see. A painting
that it must have, at the very least, cost a fortune to secure for even a single night—as she
refused to contemplate the idea that he might
have actually *bought* it.

She ran a hand over her face, unsure as to
whether she was relieved or even more upset.

'I thought…' She trailed off, unwilling to say
the words out loud.

'I know.'

She felt him come to stand behind her, the
wall of heat at her back bringing her senses to
life.

'Did you want it to be the Durrántez?' he
asked, his tone so neutral she could have
screamed.

'I don't know,' she replied honestly.

With one last look at the Gentileschi, she
turned, still unable to meet his eye. 'I ruined
this, didn't I?' she asked.

'Not at all,' he said lightly, handing her a
glass of champagne.

'You're a terrible liar,' she said, the last word
catching in her throat. She couldn't help the
tear that escaped down her cheek. A tear that
Sebastian swept away with his thumb.

The Durrántez would always be there. Coming between them. Until one of them broke. She just didn't know which of them it would be.

His thumb moved from her cheek to rest against the centre of her bottom lip, as it had done earlier that day. Instinctively, she gently bit down on the pad, anchoring it in place, desperate for anything that could connect them beyond the damn painting.

Her lips came around the tip of his thumb, so slightly sucking on it before letting him go. She turned away, still unable to make eye contact, to let him to see the shame she felt, the embarrassment that she had got it wrong. Got *him* wrong.

But his hand came up to her jaw, gently guiding her to face him. He waited for her to raise her gaze to his. If she'd expected censure, frustration or resentment she'd once again misjudged him.

Fire blazed in his eyes and it pulled open a door within her, creating a sudden backdraught of desire. A hot, twisting sensuality that she felt calling to her body from his. His eyes dropped to her lips and something wild and feminine cried out from her soul. In the days since they had first come together Sia had learned a lot about her body, her desires. He had taught her how to ask for what she wanted, how to listen to her body and know what that was. He had driven her to heights of ecstasy she could never have imagined in moments of beauty she could never have expressed to another living soul.

And after the agonising hours spent wondering and guessing she didn't want to think any more. To question any more. No, she wanted to drown in the way that Sebastian was looking at her. As if she were both his salvation and damnation.

Silently she dared him. Dared him to take what he wanted from her. To do as he willed, for as long as he willed it. She saw the moment he understood, the flare of surprise in his eyes, the sparkle of golden flecks bright against deep, dark, unfathomable eyes. His hand wrapped around her waist, drawing her chest against his. She let her head fall back in surrender, relaxing into his hold, and he feasted on her. Openmouthed kisses sent shivers radiating across her skin from her neck that she felt in her very core, as if he were already there, consuming her from within.

His hand came up to her hair, his fingers sweeping into the strands and firmly guiding her head back to his, his eyes locked on her lips again for the barest second before he claimed them for his own.

And she relished it, the powerful exploration he made of her, the press of his lips, the way his tongue filled her. She clutched at his shirt, clinging to him, wanting more from him. She felt utterly enthralled by his touch, his kisses, his command.

She was barely conscious that with one free hand Sebastian pulled the chair out from the table and walked them towards it. He positioned them in between the table and chair, pulling her onto his lap as he sat them both down.

Her chest unfurled against him as she sought to press herself deeper into him. Her gasped inhale must have pleased him as she felt his hands fist against her backside, as she drew her knees closer to either side of his hips, ensuring that she brushed up against the length of him, the hard, powerful erection leaving her in no doubt as to his desire for her.

His hands worshipped her body, tracing invisible pathways from her neck, around her breasts, over her taut nipples and down her torso and abdomen to her hips, pulling her once again against him in a way that made her want, need their clothes gone.

As if he sensed her urgency, his hands slipped beneath her dress, came up and over her thighs, his fingers hooking into the elastic band of her panties, his thumb firmly pressing against her clitoris, drawing a moan from her which he consumed with the kiss he still devoured her with. She writhed against his hand, her body shaking with need and urgency. He lifted her slightly, manoeuvring the thin strap of her panties over one leg, then the other, before returning her to his lap and casting them aside.

Her hands swept to the waistband of his trousers, making quick work of the fastening and the zip, pushing aside his boxers to feel the length of him in her hands, hot and velvety. Her thumb danced gently over the tip before positioning him beneath her as she held herself above him.

Her tongue danced with his and she risked a glance, startled to find his eyes staring into hers. She gently drew the kiss to a close, wanting to focus on him, wanting to see what he saw, to feel what he felt when she lowered herself down onto his length.

As she did she watched a hot, heady blush rise to his cheeks, saw the fierce control and concentration he was exerting over himself to allow her to take the lead in this. The way his pupils dilated to inky black depths drove her on. She held his gaze, the connection so focused it spurred her on, gave her confidence, made her want to relish the power he had given her.

She felt her muscles flex around him as the torturously slow way he filled her made her gasp again and again the lower she got, the skirts of her dress fanning out to cover where they came together, seemingly both indecent and discreet at the same time, adding a strange heady, wicked pleasure to their joining.

It wasn't long before she lost control of the devastatingly slow pace she had set, delighting in the way she could no longer tell where she ended. Her eyes drifted closed, finally severing the intense connection between them and her head fell back. Sebastian's arm came around her, allowing her to bend over it as he placed open-mouthed kisses on her breasts and his thumb swept beneath her skirts and found the apex of her thighs, pressing firm circles around her clitoris, bringing her closer and closer towards the most powerful orgasm she'd ever experienced. She wanted to tell him to wait for just for a minute, just so she could capture this feeling, this moment with him, to hold it to her and—

And then he thrust upwards into her and the stars fell from the sky, through the house, down into the basement and showered them with golden light that she consumed as she gasped air into her lungs and he pulsed within her, his own completion pouring into her making her feel more alive than she remembered ever being. And in that moment Sia knew that she would make the most of it. Whatever 'it' was, and for however long it was to last, she would see it through to the end.

CHAPTER TEN

INTERVIEWER ONE: *So, instead of making use of your time on his estate in Siena to search for the painting, you went on an art tour?*

MS KEATING: *It was Florence.*

INTERVIEWER TWO: *[whispers] Did you see David?*

'SO YOU'RE TRYING to tell me that between the Uffizi and the Galleria dell'Accademia, of all the things we saw, your favourite was the *Gates of Paradise* on the Baptistery of St John?' Sebastian demanded, staring at her with all the mock horror he could summon. Secretly he was pleased.

'Eyes on the road, mister.'

'That's Your Grace to you,' he teased, taking his eyes back to the sweeping road returning to the estate.

He'd been almost sure that she was leaving him the night he had the Gentileschi brought in. But the passion they had shared that night had been like nothing he'd ever known before. She'd surrendered to him and it had awed him—the trust she had placed in him. He wasn't sure he was worthy of it. But something deep within him had started to hope.

'Can we go back?'

'Now? Did you forget something?' he said, his hands pausing on the wheel and already scanning a turning point.

'No, I just want to see more of it. And some of it again. And that spaghetti… Sebastian, seriously, that most definitely has to be done again. So tomorrow? Maybe we could…?' The pleading in her tone was too much to resist.

'If you want to, I am yours to command.'

'Okay. But we should get up *really* early. I want to avoid the tourists.'

Sebastian couldn't help the belly laugh that erupted from his chest. 'We *are* the tourists,' he chided, and flinched as she slapped him on the arm.

'You know what I mean,' she threw at him.

'There's no reason we couldn't stay over.'

'In Florence?'

'Yes,' he said, mentally flicking through his contacts. 'We could stroll the Ponte Vecchio, have dinner on the other side of the river, looking out across at—' He frowned as his phone vibrated in his pocket and the ringtone he'd assigned his sister cut through the sound of the wind whipping past the car.

'Sorry, it's Maria. I have to take this.'

He searched for the headset but couldn't see it, immediate concern about the baby, about Maria firing in his blood enough for him to know it wasn't safe for him to be driving. Before the call could ring off, he saw a layby and pulled into it, ignoring the arc of sand and pebbles thrown into the air as he hit the brakes.

'*Estás bien?*' he demanded down the phone, as he turned off the engine and launched from the car. He knew that his reaction might be seen as extreme, but he also knew Maria. Knew how much she'd valued and embraced her newfound freedom and knew more than anything that this wouldn't be a social call.

'Yes, I am,' she replied calmly, as if having expected such a reaction. 'And you need to hear that because I really am okay, despite what I'm going to tell you.'

Sebastian took a breath, her words really not doing anything to assuage the fear he was feeling for his sister.

'I've left Matthieu.'

'What happened?' he growled.

'It's not important, but I wanted to tell you myself before you found out from someone else. I've already found a house in Umbria. It's a two-hour drive away from you—'

'I'm coming.'

'I don't want you to.'

'I don't care, I'm coming,' he said mulishly.

'Not if I don't give you the address.'

'Maria, we both know that I can find you in less than fifteen minutes if I want to,' he said. Realistically he only needed ten, but it was a Sunday.

'But you won't, because you're my brother and you will respect my wishes.'

'I'm going to kill him,' he promised through gritted teeth.

'You won't, even if I did consider letting you do it for just a minute. Because Matthieu is the father of my unborn child.'

'Come home?' he asked, knowing already that he was defeated.

'Sebastian, that's *your* home. It's time I found one of my own.'

After another five minutes of assurances that she was okay, she signed off. *'Te amo, hermano.'*

'Te amo, hermana,' he concluded, before disconnecting the call.

He stared, unseeing, at the range of dusty green hills beside the road, his hand white-knuckled around the slim phone.

'Are you okay?' Sia asked.

'No. And I won't be remotely okay until I have found Montcour and beaten him into a pulp,' he said, his anger finally taking hold, his tone harsh, his words yelled, and he cursed, throwing his phone on the ground in rage.

'Is this something you do a lot?' Sia asked from inside the car, her face turned to him, her eyes covered by sunglasses, her expression impassive.

'Qué?' he demanded, confused by her question.

'Perhaps I don't know you well enough to tell if this is your usual reaction to bad news, or if this is extreme. Either way, I can't say I'm a fan.'

'If you don't like it—' he said, the heated words coming out of his mouth before he could call them back.

'It's not a matter of like. You are beginning to scare me.'

The calmly delivered line was at complete odds with her words, but the thought that he might have been in any way making her afraid cut him like a knife. The excess adrenaline from his anger, from his need to fight for those he cared for crashed through him but he quickly got himself under control. He cast a hard glance back towards her, concerned that he had pushed her too far. As if sensing his need, Sia took off her sunglasses. The purity of her gaze, the honesty and concern—not fear—shining for him, for his sister struck him all over again.

'Your sister, is she okay?' Sia asked.

'No. She's eight months pregnant, alone and if anything happens to her—' Residual waves of helpless anger still lapped over him.

'Is she in danger?'

He forced himself to take a breath. 'No.'

Sia leaned over to the driver's seat and opened

his door, inviting him back into the car. 'What about Eduardo?'

'What about him?' Sebastian asked, utterly confused about what their father had to do with it.

'Can he do anything?'

Sebastian sank into the seat of the sports car with a bitter laugh. 'He's been the dictionary definition of absent for Maria's entire life. I doubt very much that he's going to change now.'

Sia leaned back in the leather seat, tucking her feet beneath her, signalling her patience for an explanation. He nearly laughed. Somehow, the truest interactions they shared had become silent exchanges, no need for words or questions, their understanding of each other almost instinctive.

'It was one of the conditions of the purchase of their estate in Rimini. That Maria come to live with me.'

'How old was she?'

'Eight.'

Sia nodded as if beginning to understand and perhaps, given her own parents, she might just be able to.

'It was the only way to protect her. Even before our father lost everything in the deal with Abrani, he had removed himself from her, emotionally and physically. Maria is a study of my mother. Hair, eyes, nose, mouth, chin…an almost exact replica. And, much like everything else, Eduardo simply couldn't bear to be reminded of his wife. Because my father, despite all that he became after her death, had loved her so completely in life.

'So, even though it was unintentional, I had to stand by and watch while he broke my sister's heart, knowing that I wasn't enough to fix it and never would be. Because what she needed was her father.'

Sia's heart broke, knowing just how much that would have hurt Maria. Knowing just how much it had hurt her to be separated from her own father. But it also ached for the boy who had become a parent at such a young age. Not just to Maria, but to himself. Her heart melted for the man who would clearly do anything to protect those he loved, those within his purview. She'd seen that at the hotel. She saw it every day in the little things he did for her that she had almost stopped noticing. The way he would have spun the car round and driven back to Florence. The way he had arranged for her to see everything she could ever want in Siena and Florence, and further.

But Sia could see that he was still caught in the past, pulled by the negative tug beneath a tide of anger, and she hated the hold it had on him. And the only way he could move on was to change his thinking, to shift his focus. Torn for just a moment, she realised that the risk of hurting him was not enough to outweigh the gift of release if her plan worked.

'I agree that Eduardo should have stepped up. I'm truly sorry that he wasn't capable of it. You should never have had to do the things you did. But, because you did so, could it be that Eduardo didn't *need* to?' she asked gently, bracing herself for the reaction she knew would come.

'So I should have let the whole thing crash down about our ears?' he demanded hotly.

'No. But Sebastian, it's not about shoulds, coulds or might-have-beens. You *did* step up. And because of that Maria had a safe, loving, caring brother to look out for her. Which is exactly why she's going to weather the storm she's experiencing with her husband.

'Your father had a very plush roof over his head with his wife, and you found the strength to build an international hotel conglomerate that is worth billions,' she said, infusing her voice with all her awe and wonder that he had been able to do so. 'Something that might not have happened had your father managed to resolve even half of the emotional baggage he needed in order to be there for his children. And perhaps, rather than focusing on whether that *should* have happened or not, you could focus on the amazing things that resulted because you did?'

Sebastian resisted the urge to shake off her words. For so long he'd been looking at what he'd missed, what it had cost him to compensate for Eduardo, to assume the position as head of his family. But Sia was right. When he considered what he had gained, not money or things but security, emotional and physical, for his sister and, as much as he could, for his father and Valeria and even himself, that was so much more than where they could have ended up. And the hard work that he put into his company, it had allowed him to invest in his friends, like Theo, and staff, the people who worked for him. In fact, all those early years of struggle and hardship, the impossibly long sleep-deprived hours, they had brought him here, to a moment in time where the world was his oyster—he could now do literally anything with his life. And the sense of accomplishment that spread through him, the pride in his own hard work and achievements began to smooth over the harsh hurts of the past. Not completely, but in its own way it began a healing that took him by surprise.

He cast a look at where Sia was sitting beside him and all he wanted to do was haul her into his lap. As if sensing the train of his thoughts, she smiled, pure wicked deliciousness.

'I didn't pick you as an optimist,' he said, restraining that heat before he did something ludicrous that would have them arrested for public indecency.

'Oh, I am—which is why I know I'm going to get my hands on the painting,' she teased, and he wondered if she realised it was the first time that she'd made a joke, or even referenced the Durrántez since their first night in Siena.

Keeping his hands on the wheel of the car,

and not all over her body where he wanted them, he pressed a kiss on her lips, a promise of more to come. He turned the key in the ignition and guided the car back onto the road that would see them home.

In that moment Sebastian realised that Sia hadn't asked her question since that night either. Was it because she no longer wanted to prove that he'd stolen the painting? Was that a good or a bad thing? He couldn't tell. But now he had a different perspective on his past, along with the realisation that it wasn't that he didn't want a family or commitment in his future— but that *because* of his past he didn't trust that he could ever have such a thing. But Sia was making him want it. Want it with her.

As he parked up in front of the door, Sia was almost halfway out of the car before it had stopped. 'I'm going to stretch my legs before dinner,' she said with a smile on her lips and in her eyes.

'It's not in the garden,' he teased of the painting's location.

She shrugged and turned, walking away. 'But it is here somewhere,' she called over her shoulder.

Sebastian didn't see the way the smile slowly loosened on her lips, the way that Sia steeled her shoulders and spine before removing her mobile phone from her clutch, the way her jaw clenched as she checked the fourth message from Bonnaire's on her answering machine.

'Ms Keating. This is Michael. We've been trying to reach you for quite a number of days now. We have some questions to put to you and we would like to pin down a date for you to come in and speak with our investigative team. Especially given the company you have been keeping since your suspension. We expect to hear from you in due course.'

Her hand shaking, Sia deleted the messages before turning off her phone and slipping it back into her bag. They had suspended her for thirty days. She had been away less than half that. She had five days left of the fourteen that Sebastian had given them and her heart raced at the thought that time was running out. No matter how much she might want to, she couldn't hide out here for ever.

* * *

Dressed in Sebastian's shirt and an old pair of jeans she'd found in her suitcase, on bare feet Sia made her way out into the garden to a table laden with coffee, croissants and fruit. Smiling at the half-eaten croissant and half-drunk coffee Sebastian must have consumed in haste before heading out to see Maria an hour ago, Sia unfolded the English newspaper he insisted on having delivered to the estate for the duration of her visit.

Sinking into her seat, she poured herself a coffee, picked up the cup with both hands and inhaled the rich aroma as the heat from the china warmed her palms. It was already hot and barely into double digits, today was going to be…

Her thoughts trailed off as she caught sight of the image dominating the front page of the newspaper. A large black and white photo showed a handsome couple, heads bent, as the man stretched out his hand as if both protecting the woman and warding off the press. But it was the woman who caught her eye. Because Sia had seen her before and as her eyes skated over the accompanying article, the bottom dropped out of her world.

Abrani Heiress Weds Billionaire!

Despite recent concerns over the attempted sale of a fake painting, things are beginning to look up for Sheikh Abrani as his youngest daughter Aliah surprises the world with a shock secret wedding!

Rumours about possible pregnancy are yet to be addressed by the royal family, but an official statement is expected in due course.

The Sheikh's youngest daughter might have been recently married, but less than eleven days ago she'd been sipping champagne with Sebastian Rohan de Luen, in a private club in Mayfair. 'An old family friend' he'd said, just before calling her beautiful.

Of all the people perfectly positioned to swap out the real painting for the fake, surely the Sheikh's daughter would be at the heart. Something caught in her mind, the memory of Sebastian's righteous recounting of the Sheikh's sins, the least of which was the fact Abrani had

literally gambled her hand away in marriage...
and that was considered a *good* thing.

All this time, Sia realised, she'd been focused
on Sebastian but not the people who could have
helped him—like the artist who'd created the
forged painting. In her mind's eye she was back
in David's lab, the night the fake had been damaged, scanning the painting, the remaining
brushstrokes, the technique that...that...

Her mind leapt from one painting to another,
but quite possibly by the same artist. Astou
Ndiaye, the Senegalese artist who Sebastian
had chosen to commission for his Caribbean
island hotel. Because something Sia had seen
in the two large canvases—a brush stroke, a
colour combination—something even then had
risen a flag to her visual senses and now she
couldn't help but wonder...could Astou have
been the forger? What had Sebastian called it?
A recent commission.

She reached for her phone and pulled up the
search engine. Ndiaye's website was the first
hit and she flicked across the images of her abstract paintings, but further below were a collection of classically styled paintings, portraits
and still lifes—certainly showing promise and

a strong sense of the classical techniques that would have come in handy when trying to forge a Durrántez. Clicking through to her bio, Sia's heart plummeted as she discovered that Ndiaye grew up in Senegal but went to live in France after her mother, who had been a high-profile trader, had been forced to declare bankruptcy. Right around the time Eduardo's business deal had fallen through.

A wave of anger began to build, as if a way out from shore yet but coming closer and closer the more her suspicions grew. And she almost didn't want to look further because if she was right, if what she thought was true, it might break her.

Bracing herself, she pulled up a new tab and searched for the name Sabbatino. Headlines screamed back at her, laying bare the various secret assignations of the Italian brothers, one particularly insalubrious article saw a woman proclaiming to have spent the night with both of them. Ignoring the attention-grabbing reports, she instead clicked on the few images.

Pictures of the two handsome Italian brothers grinning at the camera, suave, sophisticated, charming and doing absolutely nothing for Sia until she caught sight of one particular image. She clicked on the thumbnail and used two fingers to enlarge the image on her screen. There they were, arms slung around each other as they stood in front of their yacht. A yacht they were currently sailing around the Caribbean.

A pit yawned open in her stomach and she pushed the phone away before she could see any more. Before she could hurt any more. It wasn't the proof that she needed. It was nothing she could take back to Bonnaire's. But that didn't matter any more.

She'd always known that he'd stolen the painting but at the very least thought she'd had his respect, his promise not to lie to her. He might have been a thief but she'd thought him truthful. Honourable. She'd been such a fool.

Sebastian had told her that his life was an open book and perhaps she couldn't say that he'd lied.

Because everything he'd done had been done in front of her, even from the first moment. Aliah in Victoriana—the thief imprisoned by her father and paid with, what, her freedom? Ndiaye's paintings in the Caribbean— the forger whose mother's career was ruined, and paid off with a massive commission. And the Sabbatino brothers? Who knew what they'd got or what even their connection was to the defunct oil deal. Did it matter any more?

She was devastated by the wave of hurt as it drew closer and closer, threatening to overwhelm her. Not because of a plan that had been put in place before she'd ever laid eyes on Sebastian Rohan de Luen, but the fact that he could do it under her watchful gaze and think he'd get away with it. Was he really that cruel? Had everything been a lie? *All* of it? Or was it just the painting?

The last time she had questioned his actions she had hidden in the fantasy. But she couldn't do it again. This time she couldn't ignore what was staring her in the face.

Sebastian returned to the house just as the sun was beginning to set, feeling much better than he had for a long time. He and Maria had spoken almost all day. He was surprised to find how strong she was. Hurt, yes, and for that he would most definitely make Montcour pay. But her determination to forge a future that would protect her and her child had made him proud for her.

For the first time he had seen her as more than his little sister. He had seen her as an adult, a woman. A mother. It was incredible.

He took the steps to the house two at a time, excited and happy to be returning to Sia. He'd told Maria about her, of course. Not everything, and nothing about the Durrántez, but he'd explained that he was thinking about things differently. And he only had Sia to thank for that. He wanted to tell her, thank her for making him wait, for making him calm down. That as much as he'd wanted to step in and take control, Sia was also right in that Maria needed to do that by herself and she was flourishing.

In his enthusiasm it took him a moment to realise that the house was shrouded in darkness. Had there been a power outage? But as he headed further down the hallway he saw a light on in the corner of the living room.

He leaned against the door frame, his arm above his head, just looking at her. Curled up on a large cream armchair, her head turned to look out of the window, she was the most beautiful thing he'd ever seen. In a large oversized thick wool cardigan and soft silvery-grey lounge suit it shouldn't have worked with her golden Titian hair, but it did. She seemed regal almost, like a figure from a Renaissance painting—a silver angel with a crown of gold.

And then she turned to look at him and the sadness in her eyes cut him like a thousand knives.

'What happened? What's wrong?'

She ignored his question and asked, 'Is Maria okay?'

'Yes,' he assured her.

'Good,' she said, turning back to look out into the darkness beyond the window.

'She wants to meet you.'

Sia shook her head. 'I'm not sure that's a good idea.'

Something slithered in his stomach, making him nauseous.

'Why?'

'I have to go back to London,' she said, gently tapping her mobile phone against her knee.

'When did that happen?'

Instead of answering him, she nudged at the newspaper folded up on the table beside the lamp. While he scanned the headline, his gut clenching tighter and panic shooting through him like lightning, her gaze returned to the window.

'Did you know that the Sabbatino brothers have a yacht? And that Ndiaye once studied fine art at the Sorbonne? And that both had parents who were negatively impacted by un-disclosed business deals in the same year that you were exiled?'

There were so many ways he could have re-sponded to her question, but he finally settled on the truth. 'I did know those things, yes,' he admitted.

'What? You didn't want to know if that was my 'question' before answering it? Because it wasn't,' she said, shaking her head. 'That's coming, but not yet.'

Anger began to mix with the fear, creating a toxic concoction spreading through his veins. 'I thought we were done with that game.'

'It wasn't a game, Sebastian,' she said dis-dainfully. 'It was my job. My reputation. My career.'

He blanched. 'I can get you another job.'

'And the fact that this is your response goes

to show how little you understand what I've lost.'

'Don't talk to me about loss,' he growled. 'My family lost everything—home, money, reputation.'

'The exact price that I am paying for your revenge,' she said, her voice so horrifyingly calm. 'Do you *care*?'

'Of course I care! How can you ask that?'

She shrugged indifferently. 'Because at every turn you give me two very different sides of the coin. The billionaire hotelier who throws a VIP party for his staff. The thief who will do anything to protect his co-conspirators. The brother who was more father to his sister than anything and the playboy who almost made me love him,' she choked as a tear began to roll down her cheek.

Sebastian experienced a tearing sensation as half of him soared with joy at even the possibility of her love, but the other—the half that registered the past tense, who caught the word 'almost' and who realised the depth of her sadness—felt the greatest loss he'd ever experienced.

'How could you have done that to me?' she

demanded, unfolding from the chair and closing the distance between them. Her anger, her hurt, the thread of injustice vibrating in the air between them calling to him. 'How can you proclaim to care and yet wave *every* aspect of your thievery and falsehood in my face?'

The pain her words caused made him desperate. Unable to shake the feeling that the most precious thing he could ever know, ever touch or be near wasn't the millions and millions of pounds' worth of paintings in his basement but the woman who sat in front of him.

'You weren't supposed to be there. You *weren't*,' he insisted. 'It was supposed to be Sean Johnson, who came down with food poisoning the night before flying to see the Sheikh. It wasn't supposed to be you.'

'But it was,' she said simply. 'So my question, the one you promised to answer truthfully...' she said, piercing him with a look, warning him, begging him, and he felt it call to his very soul. 'Was it worth it?'

He flinched.

'Stealing the painting and all that it resulted in. Was it worth it?'

He reached for her then, crushing his lips to

hers in a kiss that would brand them both. For a blissful moment she unfurled beneath his touch until he felt it, the second she regained her hurt about her like a shield and pushed him away.

'Was it worth it?' Sia demanded, her voice hoarse with pain. She looked at him, breathing just as hard as him, the look in his eyes unfathomable.

'Yes—but not because of the painting,' he rushed to add. But it was too late. His words had done the damage she knew they would.

'Sia, listen to me. It was worth it because it brought you to me.'

'And you expect me to believe that?' she cried harshly.

'You have to trust me,' he begged.

'I can't!' she yelled. 'I can't trust you at all. This whole thing has been a game to you. A con. An elaborate, incredible fantasy, but ultimately a ruse. When does it end? How will I ever know if you really do care about me or if you're just trying to get away with it?'

'Sia, I care you about you so much that I'm willing to let this go and that scares me so damn much. Everything I've risked, that other people have risked for this? I would give it all up in a heartbeat if you ask me to.' A part of her didn't want to believe him. In his eyes all she could read was sincerity, but could she really take such a gamble? 'But you won't. Because you're too scared,' he accused.

'I'm not scared of you,' she insisted.

'No, but you are scared of yourself. Terrified to reach for the things that you want, that make you unique and incredible. And until you realise that, until you face what it is you truly want, accept it and pursue it, you won't stop being scared.'

'And I suppose you think that what I want is you? Is that what your words are shaped to make me feel? To make me think?' she said, the way his words had hit home making her mean. 'I was so worried about passion, about falling into the hysterical love that consumed my mother that I missed the one real likeness we share. That you're just like my father. The forger, the con-artist.' For the first time that evening she felt a clarity descend over her— as if the ice around her heart was crystal-clear and on the point of breaking.

'But the biggest con you've pulled is on yourself, Sebastian. Because it's not me who can't trust myself and my wants, is it?' His eyes flashed a warning but she pressed on, her heart raging in her chest, aching for both herself and him.

'You say you would give it up if I asked, but it's not that simple, is it?' she demanded.

His eyes darkened, gone were the golden flecks she loved so much, gone was the gentle tease to soften the blow.

'To give it up, to give me the painting, you'd need my surrender.'

'No, it's not—'

'Is that not what you're asking? For me to tell you that I love you? For me to leave Bonnaire's, to give up my career, leave London and hang on your arm? Follow you around the world while you visit your hotel empire?'

'Would that be so terrible?' he asked, his tone halfway between sincere and teasing.

'Yes, if you were just playing some game, getting me to go along with what you wanted to get away with your revenge. And if I asked the same of you?'

'What do you mean?'

'If I asked you to give me the painting, to have your surrender before mine, would you?'

He held her gaze and this time the silence spoke volumes.

'You can't give me the painting until I tell you that I love you,' she said, her voice breaking on the last words. She felt his palm at her cheek, raised her eyes to his and gently leaned into his hand.

'And you can't tell me that you love me until I give you the painting,' he returned, the sorrow in his eyes finally matching hers.

Her heart raged in her chest, crying out that she was wrong, begging, pleading with her not to do this. Everything in her felt as if it were being torn in two and she drew in a jagged breath, trying to drown out the pain.

'I have to go,' she said, her mind severing connections her heart and soul weren't ready to yet, the well of ache—a hint of what was still to come—already building within her.

Sebastian nodded, but didn't move his hand either.

When his lips met hers, as they were always going to, she opened beneath them, pulled him to her as he sought to bring her to him, the thrust of his tongue claiming her in a way so primal, so pure, she knew she would never be the same again.

The feel of him, the taste of him, she imprinted them on her mind, on her heart, even as she was saying goodbye. She allowed herself that moment to absorb the heat and passion that pressed against her, her mind lost to all but sensations, wants and needs.

Until finally their kiss drew to a close and, without looking back, Sia collected her bags and left.

CHAPTER ELEVEN

SEBASTIAN RUBBED THE centre of his chest, where a dull ache had taken up residence the moment Sia left his estate in Siena. There was nothing dull about the pounding in his head though, which at this point either required extreme numbers of painkillers or simply more alcohol. He was leaning towards the latter.

At least the latter partly managed to limit the fragments of conversations with Sia which ran on a loop in his mind. The way that sometimes he would turn his head to the seat beside him, expecting her to be there, laughing at him in that way she did.

It was as if without her in his life there was suddenly very little to it. She'd made him see that he'd spent far too long actively indulging in his desires like a child throwing a tantrum. Yes, he'd had to work hard to protect his family, Maria…but, he finally acknowledged, he wasn't forced into that position. He simply took it. And would do it all over again.

But in the last three or so years, Sia had been the only person to challenge him, to make him look at what he was doing and want to be better, do better. He'd needed to impress her, he realised now. So dramatically different to the women who had graced his bed before, almost desperate in their attempts to impress him. Oh, he wasn't naïve enough not to realise that for the most part they were either after his money or his prowess, both of which were considerably well known.

But not Sia. She had wanted him against her natural inclination. And, in doing so, had made him look at himself through her eyes, had pulled him out of his selfish hedonism and reminded him that there was more to life. That there was her.

The woman he loved.

'Did you really punch Montcour?' Theo Tersi demanded as he stalked towards where Sebastian was sitting in the garden.

'I might have done. It's a bit hazy,' Sebastian replied without surprise at his friend's appearance, his hand lifting to gesture towards the bottle of whisky on the table.

Theo came to stand before him, hands on his hips, looking both disappointed and angry at the same time. 'And you didn't let me know so that at the very least I could be here to see it?' he demanded. 'Do you regret it?'

Sebastian reared back in offence. 'He broke my sister's heart. Of course not. Even if they have now made up and are back in Switzerland.'

'And Montcour?'

'Will get over it. If I'm honest,' Sebastian said, rubbing his stubbled jaw with his thumb at the memory, 'I think he let me.'

'Punch him?' Theo asked.

'Yeah.'

'Fair.' He nodded, shrugging a single shoulder as if in agreement with how things had played out.

'I think so,' Sebastian said, pouring whisky into the glass, passing it to Theo and holding the bottle to his lips. 'Drink. You've got some catching-up to do.'

Theo took a decent mouthful of his drink.

'Before we get to the point where neither of us are able to focus, can I see it?'

'Yes,' Sebastian replied half reluctantly, hauling himself from the chair and leading the way into the living room, where he had placed the painting on the mantelpiece above the fire.

Theo came to stand beside him and they both studied the Durrántez in silence.

'So that it's it then.'

'Yes.'

'*Christos*, she looked like Maria.'

'Yes.'

'Very beautiful women in your family,' Theo observed.

Seb turned on him, and Theo raised his hands in surrender.

'Hey, I'm a happily married man, don't look at me like that,' he said, turning back to the painting. 'So. Was it worth it?'

'*Dios mio*, you too?' Sebastian demanded.

'Okay, this time I *really* don't know why you're looking at me like that,' Theo replied, the first sign of frustration written clearly across his features.

Sebastian passed a hand across his face, trying to wipe away the days of self-disgust that had gathered around him. 'It's a long story.'

'Best you get started then.'

The sun had set by the time Sebastian had told Theo all that had happened. Theo, in a strange turn of domesticity, had gathered a half decent meal together and the empty plates and coffee cups attested to the mostly successful sobering effect of the evening.

'Well, do you? Trust her?' Theo asked.

'It's not that simple,' Sebastian dismissed.

'That's a no then.'

'No, I do. It's just…' Sebastian trailed off, trying to find the right words. 'I've had only myself to rely on for so damn long.' Theo dramatically cleared his throat, and Sebastian tipped his drink towards him in consideration. 'For the most part, it's only been me. Because the trust I had in my father? That was the unknowing, unthinking, unconscious trust of a child to its parent. It was just there and when he broke that? I think he broke something in me.' Sebastian clamped his jaw against the wave of emotion that swept over him in that moment, the confession, torn from the depths of his past, almost as much of a surprise to himself as it was to Theo. 'The thought of being that dependent on someone again, I'm man enough to admit that it's terrifying. I'm not sure that I am capable of it.'

'Well, I guess you have to weigh it up. The suffering you are feeling now for what you *might* feel *if* it doesn't work out.'

'I'm not....' He was about to say *suffering* when an inner voice whispered in his ear.

Passion is a suffering that you take on yourself for what you want.

Only, rather than willingly taking it on, Sebastian had been pushing it away. Rejecting it, denying it. Denying what he truly wanted. Which wasn't the painting, which wasn't revenge. It was Sia. Only her. And if he had a hope in hell of getting what he truly wanted then he was going to have to put himself on the line.

He dropped his face into his hands, pulling at his hair in frustration. Oh, he'd been a bloody fool. The animalistic sound that emerged from his mouth was full of self-loathing and recrimination.

'There it is,' Theo said, half satisfied and more than a little patronising. 'Let it out.'

'Why do you get to be so smug?' Sebastian groused.

'I've been there.' He shrugged. 'You have a plan?'

'I think so,' Sebastian replied, staring into the flames twisting and turning in the fireplace before raising his gaze to the painting that had started it all.

Sia stared at the glowing red figures of her alarm clock and turned on her back, glaring up at the ceiling. The one-bedroom apartment had felt tiny and very, very dark since she'd returned from Siena. The minute hand ticked over and drew her closer to the interview with Bonnaire's scheduled for just a few hours' time.

She tried to call up some kind of emotion about it, but since she'd agreed to the meeting all she'd felt was numb. Which was distinctly better than the near constant ache that had sunk into her bones the moment she'd left Sebastian's estate. A dull agony had swirled in her stomach for the few days since then, ensuring that she couldn't manage to eat more than a few mouthfuls at a time.

She missed him. Terribly. Every time she

closed her eyes she could see his smile. The way he looked at her when he thought she wasn't looking. The way it felt to have his gaze, his hands, his lips on her skin. The memory of it caused an aching arousal that led only to sadness and she had cried so much that her eyes felt constantly swollen and puffy, her heart just tired of hurting.

She had given herself two days. Two days to allow herself just to feel it. In that forty-eight hours she had asked herself time and time again why she hadn't just admitted to him that she loved him. Because, she reminded herself, unlike her mother, she *did* want more, she *deserved* more. She needed and wanted to be an equal in their love.

What had he said about not being a Neanderthal? He could be attracted to her without acting on it. Well, she could love him without being cowed by it or him. But, even as she thought it, she knew that didn't feel right for Sebastian. He would never have sought to dominate her. But the painting would have always been there. Hanging over both of them. An unanswered question, the only one she had never asked.

The other way she had spent those two days was to think about what he had said about her. That she had been scared to embrace her desires, her wants. With a long, hard internal look, she'd been forced to admit that he was right. She'd spent so long, too long, being thankful for things she shouldn't have been thankful for. The job at Bonnaire's, where they had treated her with little more than grim-faced tolerance. The obscenely expensive one-bed flat in Archway that was, in reality, hideous and oppressive, just so she could commute to work. The two things combining to ensure that she had absolutely no money or time to do anything else.

On the off-chance that Bonnaire's actually still wanted to keep her on, did *she* want to stay? Time and time again over the last forty-eight hours her mind had wandered to her uni things. The sketchpad full of drawings and plans, designs for paintings she'd never completed. She shook her head. Crazy thinking. As if she wasn't already in enough debt. But, rather than giving up on that thought, Sia had tested out a few options. Maybe going part-time? Maybe an internship or finding studio space she could share? Certainly moving out of the flat would be the first move. She didn't have to give everything up in one go. She could dip her toes in first.

The alarm finally went off beside her and she forced herself into the shower to wash away the exhaustion and heat from her overactive mind.

Half an hour later, dressed not in her usual office clothes but one of the summery creations Sebastian had given her, she was ready. It was a dress that she felt not only comfortable in but also a little glamorous and it was perfect for the gentle heat of London in July.

She grabbed her purse and stepped out into the street and almost smack bang into a man in a grey suit and carrying a black briefcase.

'Can I help you?' Sia asked over her shoulder as she turned back to lock the door. 'It's just that I'm running a little late...'

'Sia Keating?'

'Yes?' she replied.

'Can I see some ID?'

'Really? Can I see yours?' she asked, offended for a reason she couldn't quite name.

'Of course,' the man—Mike Newton—said amiably, showing his work ID.

After they had exchanged identification, he left her with the briefcase, 'With the Duke's regards.'

She stood in the doorway wearing a pretty summer dress, holding her purse and a black leather briefcase that seemed more than a little incongruous—especially considering the fireworks it set off in her stomach. Her hands shook as she lifted the briefcase in both hands to inspect it.

It couldn't be, could it? Her knees threatened to give way. Not because of the exorbitant value of what she thought the briefcase might contain. Not because of what she might do with it *if* it was what she thought it was. But because of what it meant for Sebastian to have given it to her. Her heart trembled as she caught sight of the car Bonnaire's had sent for her pulling up in front of her.

Sia was shown into one of the glass-fronted meeting rooms on the fifth floor. Two men sat on one side of the table, one on the large side, balding and slightly sweaty, and the other stick-thin, tall and with a rather abundant head of dark auburn hair.

Her mind had been a whirlwind the entire

journey here and it wasn't until that moment that she realised that Bonnaire's had summoned her to the equivalent of an interrogation. On a good day there might have been something farcical about the two 'heavies' who had been sent to interview her about the painting. But Sia suddenly saw what this could have been like only weeks ago.

A junior member of staff pulled into an interview, two weeks into a suspension from a job she needed to pay bills, to pay debts, her career and future on the line…she would have said whatever they wanted her to say. Already she felt the weight of the threat hanging in the air. But, instead of making her scared, it made her angry. Angry that they thought they could do this, not just to her but to anyone they employed.

The large one gestured for her to sit in the one chair between them. She eyed it, not liking the way it would make her feel to be imprisoned between the two men at the head of the table. Instead, she politely declined and sat a few seats further up, on the side nearing the door. She was done playing other people's games. From now on, Sia promised herself, she would make her own choices and live with the consequences.

'Ms Keating, you understand that this interview is being recorded for internal Bonnaire's purposes only and that you do not need a lawyer present?'

'I'm afraid that hasn't convinced me that I don't need one,' she said lightly, relishing the new feeling of power coursing through her veins. Perhaps having a painting worth one hundred million pounds at her feet hidden in a briefcase did that to her. Or at least the possibility anyway. She still hadn't looked inside it yet.

'But you understand the statement that I have just made?'

'Yes,' she said, biting her tongue before she could accuse him of being a patronising Neanderthal.

'Then, if you would, can you please explain how you came to believe that the painting in question was a fake?'

And even though she could make everything all disappear, just by saying that she had changed her mind, that the painting had always been a fake, that she had made a terrible mistake, a proud, defiant part of her made her say, 'As I have already explained, the painting I assessed in Sharjarhere was most definitely *not* a fake.'

The two men proceeded to ply her with questions and Sia concentrated on answering them very specifically. The fact that Bonnaire's clearly wanted her to lie was making her much more determined to tell the truth. Just not *all* the truth. And she began to see how Sebastian had answered her questions not necessarily with the intent to beguile or deceive, but to protect. Protect the people who'd helped him achieve his goal, protect her to a certain extent, from exactly this situation.

'So, let me get this straight. The reason you didn't answer our calls was because you got on a plane with the man you believe to have stolen a painting from Bonnaire's and flew to the Caribbean?'

'I believe he stole the painting from Sheikh Abrani, but yes,' she clarified, strangely angry at the possessive view Bonnaire's seemed to have towards the painting they claimed never to have been in contact with.

It was strange to be recounting the last few weeks of her life to two complete strangers.

But, as she told them in as little detail as possible about her time with Sebastian, she couldn't deny how it made her feel. She had to work hard to keep the smile from her face at the memory of him trying to get her to take control of the plane, of how much he loved his convertible sports car, of his delight in her joy at being able to see such incredible art in Florence, not even to mention the Gentileschi. At how he'd encouraged her to reach for whatever it was she wanted, how he'd allowed her complete and unfettered access to him, his body and the pleasure she could find there.

'When did you get to Italy?'

While her mind almost numbly supplied an answer, she realised that while there were a hundred different ways this could end, there was only one that she wanted.

'So you spent nearly two weeks with him and during that time…did you see the painting?'

'No.'

'And you don't know where it is?'

'No,' she answered truthfully because she didn't actually know for sure that it was in the briefcase.

'Because if you did see it—'

'Which one?'

'Excuse me?'

'Well, if you mean the forged painting, then I assume that is back in Sharjarhere with Sheikh Abrani. And you surely can't mean the 'real' painting because, according to you, that was never here as I was mistaken in my valuation.'

The stick-thin man started to go a little pink in the face.

'Because any other option,' Sia continued, 'would mean that the painting *was* stolen and replaced with a forgery under the watchful gaze of Bonnaire's. And that Bonnaire's was subsequently involved in a cover-up, which at best would be seen as perverting the course of justice and at worst would involve a much deeper criminal investigation into the practices of the auction house. It could even go back years. Who knows?' She shrugged with all the mock innocence she could muster. It wasn't hard because she suddenly felt the full force of disdain for a company that was clearly as corrupt as the Sheikh himself.

'That sounds very much like a threat, Ms Keating, which could end very badly for you.

And you would be wise not to let emotions get in the way.'

Fury wound through her and for the first time, instead of shying away from it, she embraced it. 'You appear to be accusing me of becoming emotional? Well, you're right. I *am* emotional. Very, I'd say on reflection. There are quite a number of emotions running through me right now. Feelings of anger, righteousness, power, desire—desire to see justice done, even. Every single one of them not making me worse at what I do, but better.

'Just not better for you,' she stated, watching the two men become an interesting shade of puce. 'So I will be handing in my notice, effective immediately, and you will be paying me my last month's wages, in spite of the suspension. You will do this because I know, and you know, that Bonnaire's does not want me to pay a visit to the police. And,' she said, turning to the larger of the two, 'this is more than a threat. It's a promise. It is also the last time I will see you. Because next time? *You* will be the ones needing a lawyer.'

Her heart racing wildly but ecstatically, Sia left the building, her hands white-knuckled around the briefcase, feeling a kind of adrenaline high she'd never experienced before. She was thriving on a personal power she'd had no idea she possessed. Before Sebastian she would never have had the courage to do that. Everything in her knew that it was the right thing to have done. With Bonnaire's so insistent that she tell a lie to save them, they didn't deserve the painting. And she didn't deserve them.

She rushed out onto the front steps of the building, determined to find Sebastian. Not because he'd helped her to see the truth about the company she used to work for, and not because he might have given her the world's most expensive gift, but because she loved him. She'd known it for days. But she wanted *him* to know it too. Perhaps if she maxed out her credit cards she could get to Siena. A last-minute flight might cost a fortune but it would be—

She came to a crashing halt, briefcase swinging by her side.

There, parked highly illegally on a red line on Goodge Street, attracting more attention than anyone had a right to, was Sebastian Rohan de Luen, leaning against another stunning convertible sports car, hands in his pockets, hair a

bit of a mess and with a fair bit of stubble, looking every inch the disreputable playboy he was.

But he was hers.

For a second, she just stared at him. Her eyes
raked over every inch of him, searing the image
onto her mind and heart, delighting in the way
he pulled his arms from his pockets and crossed
them over his chest, as if to stop himself from
reaching for her. The way his eyes lit on her
face and not once moved, not even to the briefcase dangling at her side.

And then she felt a smile pulling at the corner of her mouth, one that seemed connected to
the endless joy, the love building in her chest. It
grew broader and broader and the moment that
he smiled back she launched across the pave-
ment, threw herself into his arms and when he
picked her up she wrapped her legs around his
waist and kissed him like she'd never kissed
before.

'I love you.'

'Dammit,' he said, his lips still pressed
against hers. 'I wanted to say it first.'

'Tough.'

'Well, I'll just have to say it more. I love you.

I love you. I love you,' he said, punctuating each one with a kiss.

'Not everything's a game, you know,' she teased as he lowered her down to the ground, but she refused to move from his hold.

'You still have the painting,' he said, his eyes still not leaving hers.

'Yes.'

'You could have given it to them if you'd wanted. I need you to know that,' he said with all the sincerity she could ever wish for, soothing away some of the hurts of their last encounter.

'Well, as you gave me the painting, I'm assuming I wouldn't have needed your permission,' she teased.

'Nope, absolutely not. I just…it's important to me that you know the painting is completely yours to do with as you wish. Because you are more important to me than the painting. Than anything.'

Her heart soared with his words and with wonder. He loved her. She shook her head a little. He'd given her so much. And the gesture that he had made, of love, of trust, that must have cost him so much emotionally, could only be matched by one thing.

'I'm not really that sure *what* painting you're talking about. Because I haven't opened the briefcase.'

'You haven't?' He pulled back, staring at her a little as if she had lost her mind.

'I didn't need to,' she said, reaching up to cup his jaw, relishing the feeling of the stubble tickling her palm. 'Whether this painting is the Durrántez, a Monet or a Pissarro, I love you and I trust you. And I want to thank you. Because you showed me that it was okay to be *all* of me. To want more, to *be* more, to be bright and shiny and powerful.' As she said the words she felt them working a magic within her. Not only knowing that they were true, but feeling it as well. 'That wanting to be more, wanting more, wouldn't make me selfish or mean, but that it would make me strong. And part of that strength is drawn from the love that I feel for you.'

Sebastian took her hand and placed it on his heart, desperate for her to know, to feel how much her words meant to him. 'And I want to thank you. You showed me how to make peace with my past, so that I could be free to make a different future for myself. A future I want to make with you. I want to have babies with you, to be a father to our children, a husband, lover and best friend to you.' Her beautiful blue eyes shone with tears of happiness and he hoped that she could feel his heart pounding beneath her palm. 'I want to fight with you, make up with you, laugh and cry with you. I'd personally prefer not to play games with you again...' he paused as she laughed '...because I'd lose. Every time. But even then I'd still die a happy man.'

Sia looked up at him, complete trust and love in her eyes, and he was humbled by it. He took the small black velvet box from his back pocket and, getting to one knee, ignoring the way people around them had begun to stop and stare.

'Will you, Artemisia Henrietta Keating, do me the greatest honour of being my wife?'

'Yes,' she replied, a happy tear sweeping down over her cheek.

Sebastian surged onto his feet, pulled her to him and kissed her with all the love he felt in his heart. It was only when the wolf whistles and cat calls intruded that he finally let her go.

'I do have one condition, though,' she said as he rounded the car to the driver's seat.

'Get in the car, Sia,' he mock-growled. He was genuinely not looking forward to the day she realised that he'd give her whatever she wanted.

'You don't want to hear my condition?' she said, her tone wicked and full of tease.

'I want to get you home so that I can make love to you. You can tell me the condition later,' he replied, loving the way her eyes widened and her pupils responded to his sensual promise.

'It's bad form to make agreements—'

He stopped her words with the first kiss of the many more they would share over the years. As Sebastian pulled away from Goodge Street, his future wife beside him and his past as a thief firmly behind him, he knew he'd stolen the most beautiful, most precious thing of all. Sia Keating's heart.

EPILOGUE

'MUMMY! MUMMY! MUMMY! Jacob is writing on the walls again,' cried Maria's youngest daughter, running into the garden where everyone was gathered.

'It's okay, my love. Auntie Sia has put special paper on the walls so that everyone can draw whatever and wherever they like there.'

Sia smiled at her sister-in-law's daughter. 'Would you like to have a go? Here,' she said, reaching for a spare set of pencils and sharing them with the girl, who looked very much like her mother and her grandmother.

'Thank you,' the girl replied and ran off to the large wooden workshop that had been built in the back of the garden for her to paint in. Sebastian had designed and constructed it the moment she'd expressed even the vaguest notion to return to her art and she was thankful each and every day for his unending support. She had returned to university to focus on the practice of her own art rather than the history and analysis techniques of others. She had built up a small but dedicated following, which kept her happy as it allowed her to find that magical line of balance between enjoying and delighting in her family *and* her passion for painting.

Sia couldn't help but laugh as Theo Tersi played out an invisible sword fight with his daughter and Sia and Sebastian's son Jacob. Lord knew where the other two of her sons were, usually hiding up a tree or swimming in the lake.

'I don't know how you do it with three boys,' Princess Sofia of Iondorra said.

'And I have no idea how you run a country,' Sia replied with a laugh.

'Oh, that,' Sofia said, swiping the notion away with her hand. 'I have people to help me with that.'

Ella came rushing over to her mother and pulled on Sofia's elbow, holding her hand in front of her mouth. 'Mummy,' she said in the loudest whisper, 'why is there a briefcase on the wall above the fireplace?'

Sofia looked up at Sia, and Maria looked at Sofia, each of the women smiling.

'It is a game Uncle Seb and Auntie Sia are playing.'

'What's the game?'

'Not to open the briefcase,' Sia replied with a smile.

'That doesn't sound like much of a game,' Ella said, frowning and then running off.

'I think it's crazy,' Sofia replied with a smile. 'Aren't you ever going to open it?'

'I don't need to.' Sia laughed.

'So the painting stays in the briefcase, hanging on the wall above the fireplace *like* it's a painting. A—' she dropped her voice to a real whisper, leaning forward '—one hundred million pound painting?' Sofia leaned back. The look in her eyes definitely said she thought they were crazy.

'I think it's romantic,' stated Maria firmly.

'You do?' asked Sia, relieved. 'I've not asked before, because I was worried you might—'

'I don't need to see the painting. It...brought you to Seb, *and* to us, that was all I needed it to do,' Maria said.

So much had changed in the last six years. Bonnaire's had gone down in a hail of public scandal after several more dodgy deals had brought the attention of both Interpol and the British police. Abrani had been quietly removed from his position as leader of Shajarhere and the state had welcomed a new leader whose interest was focused on the betterment of his people.

Sia and Sebastian had made Siena their home, despite still travelling around the world to visit his hotels, but less frequently than he'd used to. Sebastian had taken a step back from his company to develop the vineyards at the back of their estate as well as working with a local architecture firm to explore eco-friendly social housing. He'd come to realise that he'd really loved the design aspect of his hotels and was enjoying exploring it in a way that could benefit the local community.

Sia felt a kiss pressed between her neck and shoulder and turned to find her husband's lips, eager to feel them on her own.

'Matthieu has invited us to Lake Lucerne next month.'

'You'd like to go?'

'Yes, I think he has a business proposal he wants my advice on.'

'Of course. Though it may be my last flight

for a while,' she confided, one hand on his cheek and the other taking his and placing it on her stomach.

Sebastian's eyes widened with excitement. 'Really?' he said, the joy beaming from his heart straight to hers.

'Four? *Four?*' Theo demanded, joining the table.

'They're like rabbits,' teased Maria.

'You can talk,' Sofia teased Maria as Matthieu approached, looking like a giant with giggling children hanging off every limb.

'Who are like what?' he asked as everyone fell into laughter about him.

They sat, talked and ate long into the beautiful summer's evening, Sia feeling not only at peace with the love in her heart and the child growing within her, but excited by it. Her life had become something wondrous, bright, bold and beautiful and unknowingly she glowed with it.

She caught Maria staring and nudging her brother. Sebastian turned to Maria and then to Sia.

'What?' Sia asked, unaccountably feeling goosebumps rise over her skin.

'You look like her. Not physically, but there's something about you,' Maria replied with a smile, a glint in her eye both sad but full of joy.

'Like who?'

'A *Woman in Love*.'

* * * * *

LET'S TALK
Romance

For exclusive extracts, competitions
and special offers, find us online:

f facebook.com/millsandboon

◉ @millsandboonuk

🐦 @millsandboon

Or get in touch on 0844 844 1351*

For all the latest titles coming soon,
visit millsandboon.co.uk/nextmonth

*Calls cost 7p per minute plus your phone company's price per
minute access charge

Want even more
ROMANCE?

Join our bookclub today!

'Mills & Boon books, the perfect way to escape for an hour or so.'

Miss W. Dyer

'Excellent service, promptly delivered and very good subscription choices.'

Miss A. Pearson

'You get fantastic special offers and the chance to get books before they hit the shops'

Mrs V. Hall

Visit millsandbook.co.uk/Bookclub and save on brand new books.

MILLS & BOON